W9-AVO-888

DISCARDED

THE SIEGE
OF WONDER

THE SIEGE
OF WONDER

MARK S. GESTON

DOUBLEDAY & COMPANY, INC.
GARDEN CITY, NEW YORK
1976

All of the characters in this book
are fictitious, and any resemblance
to actual persons, living or dead,
is purely coincidental.

Library of Congress Cataloging in Publication Data

Geston, Mark S
The siege of wonder.

I. Title.
PZ4.G379Si [PS3557.E83] 813'.5'4
ISBN 0-385-11359-5
Library of Congress Catalog Card Number 75–36624

First Edition

'I desire no other monument than the laughter of the madmen I have caused to be set loose upon the universe . . .'

> From the testament of Ahman al-Akhmoriahd, fifth century of the Holy City, written in anticipation of the battle at Quetez (Heartbreak Ridge)

THE SIEGE
OF WONDER

The man was young and thought: they have named this war too grandly, as they have named this place, the Holy City. He reconsidered: but it should at least be denominated as "holy" with a small *h*, for it is choked with tombs and cathedrals, mosques, shrines, places of adoration and prayer, sacred groves, enchanted grottoes and temples of nameless ritual. Priests were as common here as he remembered soldiers and technicians to have been in his own home cities before he left. Their silken and sackcloth robes bracketed the dull tans and greens of the common folk. Some were indistinguishable from princes in the richness of their garments; pearls and diamonds were sewn in swirling patterns to the hems of their cloaks, their saddles inlaid with mother-of-pearl and silver, and their escorts often rode gryphons or lithe pegasuses, as suited the varied tones and nuances they wished to lend to their powers.

The Holy City had named it the Wizards' War, as if it had already been won and enshrined in its history. It had been going on for almost seven hundred years when Aden left his home, and was known there only as "the war," as were all the wars of his people's history during their prosecution.

He stepped from the road and balanced on the edge of a marble fountain while some exalted personage thundered by with his retainers; they were all dead men, which showed their leader to be powerful indeed. Flashes of ivoried bone glinted through seams in their golden armor. The dust their horses kicked up became gold too.

Aden held himself against the fountain's rim and easily hid his disgust with the funereal cavalry; he had seen much worse. Outwardly, he mirrored the awe and reverence of the other people on the narrow street. Certain mages, it was widely known, often allowed the dust of their passage to remain gold and diamond chips, instead of transmuting back into dirt, as a reward to the people for their acclaim. Many were that extravagant. Of course, there were others who loathed such obsequiousness, so one had to be careful not to overplay the role.

Aden watched the party with his left eye. An adept mage could have detected millimetric variations between the pupil dilation of that eye and his other, just as he could have discovered the coldness and conductivity that underlay the left side of his skull. But in three years, Aden had been careful never to give such persons any reason to look.

The crowd solidified behind the party. Trading and haggling resumed. The noise, if anything, was worse than it had been before, as each person sought to compliment the magnificence of the magician's dress and his house's livery to his neighbor. The men of power in that part of the world often kept spies in their pay, some human and some otherwise, and there remained the hope of washing one's clothes that evening and finding the gold still gold at the bottom of the tub. At worst, it assured one that the magician's disfavor would not be incurred.

Aden brushed some of the dulling gold dust from his coarse tunic and, as if pondering the magician's greatness, put his smudged left index finger up alongside his nose. His eye watched the dust in the act of its transmutation, sucked dry its spectrums, counted and weighed the opaque interchanges of electrons and subatomic particles, and caught traces of the fading resonances that tied it to the wizard's mind.

The information was transmitted through the wires implanted in his skull, neck and torso, and was transcribed onto spheres of frozen helium, suspended by undetectable magnetic fields in titanium cylinders inside his ribs. The natural conductance of his skin also carried quick and subtle messages as his eye spoke directly to the spheres and to the other augmenting devices that were scattered about his body.

Aden ran his hand idly along his neck and chest; this concourse between eye and mind and torso itched. Presumably, his scratching had not distorted or confused the messages.

Aden had been in the Holy City for a month watching, and he felt the weight of his observations pressing against the interior limits of his comprehension. The balls of helium, frigid, unitary, utterly pure, rotated as miniature universes inside of him, informed by the eye, consoled and spoken to by the hybrid creature of his nervous system. The living dead, the dying life, the constant shiftings and transmutations of substance and reality, the extraordinary *inwardness* of this world, all taken from the minds and imaginations of its men of power, recompressed by the devices of the Special Office, and then jammed into the cramped spaces of his brain, to wait for the monthly block transmissions, when the Office's satellites fearfully skirted the western horizon and he could rid himself of its terrible density. Aden cowered before the knowledges accumulating inside of him, and, therefore, before the wizards. In this fear, he joined the rest of the people who had allied themselves with this and the other Holy Cities. It was so vastly different from . . .

He had trouble remembering.

. . . from the precise night of his own world.

The itching stopped, Aden imagined he could tell when the electrical currents had finished inscribing the new paragraphs on the gaseous spheres.

He pulled his jacket tightly about his shoulders. He had been standing by the fountain for half an hour since the magician had passed by. A few merchants in sedan chairs of satinwood and horn passed along the street. While he thought about his interior circuitries, the eye stirred casually and discerned what it could of their wealth and what they reflected of the economic strength of the Holy City. Such considerations meant nothing to the men of power, and Aden's world knew it, but they still insisted on looking, as if they wanted to find a common ground of normality in the way the wizards fought their war.

These were exercises that might have been carried out by any spy, trivial compared to the recordation of the passing magician and his retinue: transmutation, his personal triumph over death flouted before the people, his unarticulated powers outlined by a perceptible nimbus surrounding his head and chest. These were proper challenges for the capabilities of Aden's eye.

He had to think that, he realized during the first month of his mission, in order to remain functional. Anything less and he would succumb to the same spell that half of the world had already fallen under. Either that, or he would unconsciously betray the curious arrogance that characterized the proponents of each side in the face of the other, the defensive contempt each cultivated toward the other's conception of the universe. He would dwell constantly upon any conceit or belief that would help hold in his delicate and poorly defined equipoise between half-knowing and half-believing.

His mission had been conceived after the philosophers and scientists of his home had, after centuries of war, hit upon the difference between science and magic. Before their realization, the ritual of two worlds shadowboxing across mutually contradictory and invisible frontiers had exerted a certain fascination on both sides. Neither side understood the manners or methods of the other, and so the commonly perceptible forms of sheer movement often obscured the strategic realities of power and death.

Inevitably, through all the badly aimed attempts at attack and occupation, the two incompatible universes overlapped. The massacre at Thorn River had been the last such meeting. Before that had been the battles of The Corridor, Morgan's Hill, Kells, the Third Perimeter, Heartbreak Ridge, the Lesser Bennington Isles, Black Cat Road . . . endlessly fractured dreams through which each world sought to preserve its visions of divinity against those held by the enemy.

Those strange times, before the understanding by Aden's world, gave rise to stranger nations and personalities. Science was often confused with magic, as it had been during the latter's first death and the former's birth. Thus arose successions of intentionally equivocal and elusive intelligence and counterintelligence organizations in each world, such as the one Aden worked for, some maintaining so precarious a balance between the universe that they tried to protect and the one they attacked that they spent their whole existences fighting themselves, awarding their own agents decorations when they killed their comrades and erecting monuments to the failure of gallant, purposely suicidal missions. Thus also, the weird romance of the war itself and of the literatures it spawned.

But no one in Aden's home could find anything in the war sufficiently romantic or fascinating enough to dull their grief and sorrow. Instead of composing heroic romances, illuminated by artists (who, it was reported, were often driven selectively insane by their patron magicians in the hopes their talents would reach peaks not otherwise attainable), the men of Aden's home thought more and more deeply upon the nature of their enemy. At last they conceived that their own dreams, those which they retained, were, in the very texture of their construction, tied to objective understanding. Magic and science alike, when they strove against each other, hypothesized similar accomplishments and ends. It was in the methods that they differed.

Science could be understood and therefore controlled. The mechanisms and the sources of its power would be subject to a final switch, accessible to any man, or to any trained ape or dolphin for that matter.

Magic, as it gradually defined itself in the funereal hazes over the Burn, Devils' Slide, Cameron and two hundred other disasters, could never be understood. By its very definition, it had to remain no more objective than art. Its practice must always be intuitive, given only to persons chosen by unknowable entities according to secret elections.

From this proceeded the comparative dullness of Aden's world, and also its tired grace, its acknowledgment of universal things, universal weariness, universal frustration, universal defiance. Contrawise, it also explained the awesome personalities

the enemy's world had thrown up, with their barely pro-
nounceable names and tangled genealogies, interwoven with
beings of questionable humanity. Their world blazed with baroque, liquid fires, while the men of Aden's world concerned
themselves with blackout curtains and light beams so perfectly
coherent as to be invisible unless one was their target. The magicians paraded in raiments stitched with gold and silver thread,
studded with precious stones, costuming themselves more gorgeously than the inhabitants of myths, for they conceived themselves to be made of the same stuff. It was easy to become lost in
their world, when one's own offered so little to stand against it.
There was a damp warmth about the magicians' kingdoms that
hung about their places and works like the intoxicating sweat of
lovers.

Aden's world dressed in white: starched, spotless, undistin-
guished except for cut and tailoring, which sometimes showed
obsessive attention to detail. Almost by way of petulant counterposition, Aden's world became progressively colder and abstracted. Everything must be understood, and they found it an
unexpectedly easy step; they had always secretly believed that
everything could be reduced to component parts of the utmost
simplicity, if sufficient energies were devoted to their study.

The men of power wrapped the world in silks and incense,
which hid the poverty of their feudal society and cushioned the
jarring discordancies of pleasure and horror that it contained.
That, too, formed part of their world's charm.

Three hundred years before Aden's birth, the nations of his
world had begun to replace their guns and missiles with antennas
of increasing subtlety and precision. The computers grew to
process the accelerating influx of information that they stole
away from the hidden kingdoms. New inquiries and postulates
proposed themselves and more antennas, satellites and robot reconnaissance ships were built to confirm or deny them. Most
were destroyed; their lubricants were turned to powdered diamonds, air suddenly ceased to flow faster over the tops of their
airfoils then it did underneath, finite masses were subjected to
infinite stresses.

But enough of the devices survived to feed the computers and the persons who habitually dressed in white. These people sat before the readout consoles and blackboards in underground bunkers, refining their inhumanity, drawing further away from the wild vitality that had murdered so many of their fellows; their hands were the color of pale marble, veined with red porphyry.

They learned. Within the aching sterility of their silences, the content of magic was reduced to philosophical syllogisms, then to historical commentaries, then to equations.

The first breakthrough, after the initial realization of the difference between science and magic, was in the discovery of multiple spectrums, paralleling the electromagnetic along which all forces and presences had been previously thought to manifest themselves. The electromagnetic spectrum, it was discovered, did not extend indefinitely. At one end, it stopped with the attainment of absolute zero; at the other, it consumed itself in the high-energy situations that comprised the non-dimensional cores of black holes.

By accident and tradition, the wizards had intruded into the parallel spectrums and manipulated them through the sheer force of their possibly divine personalities. Thoughts of a particular nature that coincided with certain gestures and tones of voice granted them access into the parallel spectrums, even though they had not the slightest idea that that was what they were doing.

Propelled by the inertia that the idea of absolute understanding carried with it, the enemies of magic also entered upon the parallel spectrums, not merely blundering across their lines by a gesture and remembered set of mental attitudes preserved and taught for centuries, but quite deliberately invading them, coursing up and down their twisting limits on forces of inflexible constancy. They found they could turn the gold back into dust at will.

The horror that lurked in this was ignored during the first grand decades, when men found that they could strive against and sometimes defeat the nightmares and beauties that the magi-

7

cians hurled against them. Then it was revealed that Heisner and his staff had found that love was explainable through the application of simple equations to specific portions of the electromagnetic spectrum and the next two that paralleled it. The equations were the thing that people really felt. It was not a simulation. It was an explanation of a given phenomenon in objective terms adaptable to any time and place.

Heisner was elected to the Royal Academy for his achievement, but committed suicide before his formal installation.

The Discovery, as the histories generically referred to Heisner's finding and those that followed, cast an unexpectedly ominous tone onto the new way the war was being waged and, many said, won. The men of Aden's home began to wonder what the universe might look like when they had understood all of magic and all the forces and emotions it had controlled. Magic was art; it lived and died within each individual who practiced it. When a young person sought to know its manipulation, he started with the same fundamentals and elementary skills that his teachers had. In the understanding of numbers, stored and locked inside computers, engraved inside spheres of helium, time meant less; each man stood on the shoulders of his predecessors, gifted and condemned to a more complete span of vision.

They looked, and the ones that came after them looked. Deeper mysteries solidified into geometric masses, the gesturing sweeps of the wizards' arms were quantified into series of parabolas and their radii plotted on spacetime graphs of infallible precision.

The tangle of grid antennas and tropospheric scatter units outgrew the walls of barbed wire upon which the skeltons of hooded basilisks and minotaurs had bleached for centuries. But the suspicions that Heisner had confirmed grew also. The war cooled. Magic, half in fear and half in self-fascination, turned in upon itself, cultivating stranger and more bizarre talents. Its lands were stalked by impossibly shaped beasts; death and life were toyed with by the men of power as if they were flower arrangements, to be composed according to their personal aesthetics.

Aden had known this history when he had begun to work for

the Special Office at fourteen. By the time he was sixteen he knew part of what it meant.

When he was eighteen, he was trained, modified, his abilities at analytic thought surgically blunted, and he was sent against the enemy.

He stepped into a side street paved with glazed turquoise bricks. The houses leaned high above him; some had beautiful rugs hung from their upper balconies, out of thieves' reach. His left eye searched the glowing patterns as they shifted heavily in the late sun, his natural eye keeping pace, covering; the eyes of the Holy City were numerous and often as perceptive as his own. He searched through conjunctions of arabesques, twisted vines, heroic battle scenes and erotic myths until he found one with a triskelion of three armored legs, bent as though running. From a distance of thirty meters his eye could see that each foot had a spur tipped with a six-pointed star.

His chest itched underneath the lice in his shirt. He adjusted his clothes to seem presentable and walked into the shop below the rug. The man inside had been waiting for him for seven years.

The air inside was thick with fragrances and the hushed, careful idiom the City's men of commerce often affected. Everyone except for Aden and the serving boy was well dressed. From the cut of their robes, several might have been high civil officials or apprenticed mages. Some turned to him when he entered, but then looked away with cultivated disinterest. The serving boy refrained from bringing him the customary glass of mint tea.

Aden wandered about the shop, examining the less expensive rugs and making what he hoped were appropriately respectful noises as he passed by those of better quality. The very finest, he knew, would not be on display for they had some intrinsic magic woven into their patterns.

At length, the shop emptied. With the evening, the greater wizards of this City and the other towns that thought themselves Holy would be abroad on their chosen work and not on parade for the adoration of the rabble.

The owner sent his attendants home and then turned to Aden.

9

He was fat and rather older than Aden had expected. Half his face had been burned away by some kind of fire. A flap of skin skirted the edge of his right eye, crossed a scar line and then angled downward over part of his mouth. His words were partly masked by it, as if he were speaking from behind a confessional screen.

Aden bowed in respect to the man's rank and deformities, but then raised himself and looked directly into the other's face. The Office's eye evaluated the man's retinal pattern and found a grid of synthetic sapphire implanted there; nothing obtrusive or complex, but useful for vision in the far infrared and ultraviolet ranges. There was, therefore, no need for the password he had been taught.

Aden smiled as lightly as he could at the remains of the man's face. "I imagine . . ."

The other let the right side of his mouth drop and abruptly held up his hand; it, like his face, was scarred and half obliterated. "I cannot help you."

Aden hesitated a bit. "You are Donchak?"

"I am."

"And the rug, the one with the runnning legs, that's yours too? Is it not?"

The other man nodded politely, but his right eye stayed directed toward the floor. "It is the Office's, as is the eye that recognized it." He said this in the consciously ornate merchant's speech. He had, Aden reminded himself, been sent in over seven years ago to wait for the training of a person such as himself to be completed, the undesigned equipment tested, and the cover established by his own years of wandering through the kingdoms of magic. Still, he had hoped for a guarded wink, or something like "Thank God you've come, Carruthers."

"I imagine . . ." Aden began again.

"I understand," Donchak countered, "and I understand too much besides that. That is why I cannot help you." His half-face was arranged in planes of sadness. "You are too late for my help. Please go."

"With the eye?" Aden suppressed a twinge of confusion. For

all its wonders, the eye was feeling more and more like a detonator, threatening to ignite unstable elements both in the City and within his own mind. "I can't stay here with it grafted onto me. You must know that even the small amounts of energy it leaks and the block transmissions can't go unnoticed forever."

"Then leave."

"It's shielded here." Aden heard himself getting impatient. "The mass of energies and spells. The air's so thick with them that it's a wonder anyone can breathe. The only way I got it this far is because it didn't start working and sending until I was through the borderlands and into the middle of this lunatic nation . . ."

"If you feel that way, you must correct the problem yourself." Donchak brought his left hand up and covered the erased portions of his face, further softening the sound of his words.

"Were you betrayed?" In desperation Aden shifted the conversation back against the man.

"Only by myself."

"But this shop? You must be fairly well off."

"The building is mine only so long as I remain the private joke of some men of power. They view it in the nature of a game to occasionally pit their arts against my desire for understanding them." Donchak looked around him. "My rugs are also reputed to have some abilities of their own, which one properly trained could use."

Gone native, thought Aden, and more than a little crazy too. "But you mean the rugs that you sell. The weavers . . ."

". . . are blind, as tradition specifies. That is correct, as am I." Donchak smiled at Aden for the first time. "That is my one secret from them. My eye is blind, but the last apparatus the Special Office gave me that I kept still lets me see into areas few of them care exist."

"Your patterns, then . . ." Aden's words trailed off as he thought that Donchak must be seeing him as a dancing glow of cobalt, saffron and orange.

Donchak's fractional smile continued. "Simple understanding of the interrelation of the chromatic, spatial and auditory spectra and the responses that can be coaxed from their various combinations." The man could still talk, at least, in the language of the Office. The abstractions of Heisner's successors sounded out of place among the rugs and gilt work of the shop's interior.

Outside, muezzins sang warnings to the City and to their masters' enemies. They vied with each other in the lyric intricacy of their threats, each seeking to exceed the one before him in describing the horrors that waited those who opposed his master's designs. The civil government abandoned the City at dusk and retired to its barracks and offices.

"Are you watched?"

"Tomorrow I shall be. If you are still here tomorrow, I shall be questioned too." Donchak began walking away. "There are spy entities here, and there and there." He pointed with his flabby arms at points in the air as he walked. "I have masked their sensitivities. At any rate, I presume that they will not be looking in the areas where your eye's power drain could be detected. But they see you are here and probably discern that I am talking to you, though they cannot understand the words. Please go."

"But the war. The Office cannot . . ." Aden had spotted insubstantial stains of light hovering in the places that Donchak had gestured toward. He felt his throat and stomach tighten.

"I cannot afford to concern myself with either."

"Myself, then?"

"I know nothing of you. You were a child when I was modified and sent in." Donchak paused, resting his hand on the silver tea service. "You can stay if you choose, if you judge you can hide from my companions"—he waved again to the spy entities. "Wait until the effects of the Office's surgeries wear off and use your understanding to make a place for yourself. It's more than you'll be allowed to do if you reach home again." Donchak continued to stare at him, his eye moving in minute arcs across his body as it gauged the temperature differentials between veins and arteries, and perhaps deciphered the electric crown of wires buried in Aden's skull, reading his fear.

"Then I'll betray you." Intending to be coolly threatening,

Aden over-controlled and the words came out brittle and hinting at irrationality.

"I have told you that the men of power know . . ."

"They do not know of your eye, only your mind."

"They have not thought it worthwhile to look beyond my mind."

"But wouldn't they be disturbed to know that some of the powers they've bought, however slight, came from graphs that you learned in a secret police school, or that the patterns that so please their women . . . ?"

"They probably already know."

"If they did, you wouldn't be here. They'd permit your training and your former allegiance, but not that grid. That would be too much. They'd take it from you before they found themselves asking you what you saw with it, as if you were some kind of mirror they couldn't resist looking into. And if they take it from you . . ." Aden shrugged theatrically, only later thinking that Donchak saw his fear and not the gesture. "If you consider yourself a joke now, Donchak, think how their powers of illusion will eat at your understanding when you're left in the dark." Aden felt almost proud that he should have thought of such a tack to use on the other man; it was fortunate he had studied the man's psychological profile before he had been sent in. "Anyway, they cannot be ignorant to what has, or has not been going on. They're edgy and nervous with the way the war has been going."

"But we aren't?" Donchak whispered icily.

Aden ignored him. "That's why they've been going at each other even more than usual lately. All that dammed-up ability and power. They don't dare use it, because that would give the Office and the Border Command and Lake Gilbert a chance for more study."

"Study their power? Had they not studied it enough at Thorn River?"

"That was important. It added a great deal . . ."

"But didn't they see enough?" Donchak drifted on in the same remotely irritated tone. "I was there, you know. The thing that the Office had put into this eye"—he gestured toward the scarred side of his face—"was like what yours must be now. I was caught there and, unlike the others, I could see the magicians coming through the sky and striding across the plains to crush us."

Aden let the advantage of his argument slip away as he listened. Thorn River had been among the last great engagements between science and magic, and the largest to have occurred in his lifetime. He remembered, for an instant, the streams of starved and brutalized refugees that had passed his home for days, heading for the sanctuaries of the Taritan Valley, and thought he found Donchak's face among them.

"And I could see the Border Command ships circling it during the first three days. I could see the masses of attack planes and bombers that waited behind them, waited for three more days, three more hours, three seconds while another variation of the magicians' power was expended on someone, picked apart and catalogued. I saw the face of the wizard that burned me, and I saw the face of the man who examined it and hoped for my death because that would tell him even more about the magic. I even remember their names, though I cannot say the wizard's with the way my mouth is now. The man's name was Etridge." Donchak paused for a moment. "Do you truly want your eye to serve people such as that, people who could watch such things as if they were lessons drawn on blackboards?" Donchak seemed to be genuinely amazed with his own question, as if its articulation had preceded his thoughts and accidentally proposed something that he would not have otherwise considered possible.

"Of course. They're not monsters."

"They watched, cold and bloodless. They did nothing when they might have stopped it, or at least drawn their enemy away. Is that not something worse than simple monsters?"

"Not at all. They were pursuing a"—Aden found the words coming with more difficulty than he would have wished—"a duty. That was the only thing they could do if we were to get anywhere."

Donchak fixed him suddenly with his functioning eye. "There

were other ways! A hundred other ways. Mine, the Office's, the regular services', the Academy's."

"It worked. It's working now. Look at what happened to them at Foxblind."

Donchak softened his voice; his eye returned to looking at the floor. "The price was excessive, wouldn't you say? Thousand and hundreds of thousands at Thorn River, myself, the killing of this." He swept his hand toward the door.

"This? The City?" Aden forced outrage back into his voice; Donchak was playing on treasonous grounds again, Aden's.

"There is not enough beauty here for you?"

"Beauty destroying itself."

"If it tried to understand itself thoroughly enough to defeat us, to fight us according to our own rules, it would no longer be beauty. It would just be numbers and knowledge, circling round its own grave. Do you want that?" he asked again.

"I must," Aden said at once, but did not know where the words had come from for he had not felt his tongue move.

Donchak waited for a moment and then nodded, either to the younger man's threat or to the logic of his position. The muezzins finished their arias. Aden glanced through the door-grill and his eye picked up auroral waverings in the gaps between the houses. He saw the distorted reflections of other lights on the glazed paving stones. The mages often said they were practicing their arts for their own perfection and in preparation against the other half of the planet. The fact that they practiced so often and so enthusiastically on each other spoke for itself.

"Where am I to leave this?" Aden pointed to his left eye. "The Office must have a place that is mobile, if at all possible, and protected."

"I am aware of the Office's wants and needs." Donchak muttered and walked toward the back of the shop. A barred door led out to an alleyway.

They left the perfumed rug shop and the stench of the City closed over Aden again. The paving stones were fired turquoise, even in the alley, but the piles of filth and garbage behind each building dulled the reflected light of the magicians' practice.

They passed three brave, or particularly hungry figures digging into the trash heaps. The spectrographic abilities of Aden's eye informed him that at least one of them was a leper.

The City had been named Cape St. Vincent before the war. Then the wizards had come to it and brought their reborn powers and mysteries with them. Within a decade after they had consolidated their rule over the area, they had grown powerful enough to send away the ocean that had faced the city, because it displeased them. The old city's marble quays and granite boulder jetties still surfaced from under newer buildings only a century or two old. With either marvelous whimsy, or, more likely, invincible blindness, the wizards had often built on and around these structures. Aden saw one house that was partially supported by a corroding rolling derrick that one of the first engagements for the city had welded solid; his eye traced the crane's outlines in the facing wall and he thought it to be more of a superimposition of distinct worlds, rather than a single structure.

The geometric grid of the original city had dissolved into a tangle of wandering streets and alleys. This, the men of power often declared, more aptly expressed the subtlety and complexity of their personalities. The men of power regarded it as a great humanizing process, an affair of the spirit as much as anything else. Aden's world watched the process in aerial photographs and regarded it as retrogressive, chaotic, medieval.

Aden speculated how the leper would have regarded the matter. He, personally, had not noticed any great disparity in the number or character of the garbage piles in the cities of either world.

Donchak's eye led them easily through the night streets. Ironically, Aden's more versatile unit was often confused and blinded by the reflected energies that the City's wizards were playing off the ionosphere.

The avenues broadened and straightened themselves. The closely packed houses and shops gave way to the barred entrances of substantial mansions, government buildings and the great halls of the City's guilds. Many were left over from the ages when there was but one reality on the planet, and they were defined by straight lines and euclidean masses. The structures of magic had overgrown and smothered them, like the crane, with intricate masonry and marble traceries. Eccentric balconies, turrets, minarets, arches, colonnades and porticoes softened the old, harsh outlines; mosaic overlays glittered in the wizards' lights.

He was aware of the City's splendor in spite of the darkness. In Aden's home, when men chose to care, they concentrated on the definition of whole, integrated units. Their processes of understanding allowed for little else but the finishing of broad sweeps of brushed steel or oiled hardwood. Straight lines always ended cleanly or merged into precisely defined arcs and parabolas, always so complete that a building, and sometimes an entire block or town might be seen, weighed and comprehended with a single glance. This aesthetic had been pursued with such single-minded devotion that Aden had come to believe that it was as much an expression of his world's hatred for magic's passion as it was an affirmation of its own beliefs.

Aden shook his head as he walked to free himself of these thoughts. In everything he saw and remembered, there was such perfect counterposition. The devastated middle ground had narrowed, allowing each kingdom to press more closely against the other, compacting their energies until each was immobilized by its own fury. The worlds orbited each other, duplicating the death-cycles of stars, until they might become the equivalents of black holes, self-sustaining fields of annihilation.

After years in the enemy's land, he could still be shocked by this. Working for the Special Office meant that he had to keep himself suspended between the two worlds. Too much understanding and he would give himself away to the men of power or their spies; too much belief and he would come under the spell of the world. It was a difficult balancing act, no matter how much insulation the Office's surgeons and psychologists had provided. Donchak had apparently failed in this balancing, though Aden could not say upon which side he had fallen; perhaps on both, and he was being gradually pulled apart like a rope of potter's clay, becoming thinner and thinner until he broke.

Donchak slowed and pointed the way across an immense plaza. Aden's eye read the other man's skin conductance, temperature, pulse rate and blood pressure. He was tense and very agitated, but that was understandable considering their exposed position.

There was a large building across from them, set apart from the others that bordered the square and topped with onion-shaped domes. Mages' light burst across the sky from the left and the strange wavelengths of its luminescence struck against them. The eye mapped alternating serpentines of gold and silver leaf, their twistings separated and defined by raised borders of rock crystal.

Minarets, taller than anything else he had seen in the City, were posted at the building's corners; their upper portions were made of pierced stonework and both of his eyes could see the mage-light through them. There were subtler fires glowing inside them, too, near their peaks; some his right eye could pick up, while others were visible only to his left.

Aden nearly stepped out into the plaza, but Donchak threw out his arm and drew him back into a recessed gate. A quiet gray structure four stories high loomed behind the wrought iron gate. It was covered in halfhearted mosaics and heroic friezes that did little to enliven its studied dullness; another remnant of the old days, probably inhabited then, as now, by the local government.

Aden looked back to the plaza. His left eye immediately became entangled in a ragged interference pattern of the sort he had not seen since it had been calibrated by the Office's scientists and theologians. He wondered if the trouble might be with his own circuits, but his vision remained clear along its peripheral limits. The eye, the spheres of helium and the wire net buried in him conversed among themselves, exchanging small, professional tricks they had picked up during the past years. Eventually his vision resolved itself upon a unicorn.

Donchak whispered the name of a man of power. "That is his cavalry," he breathed.

"Only one?" Aden found his voice strained.

"No need for more."

It moved with such deliberate smoothness and grace that Aden speculated if that might not be the only way the creature could contain its own power. Sudden movements, unnecessary gestures, unguarded turnings of its limbs might accidentally release the energies penned up inside.

The unicorn had a short caparison of electric blue on which were sewn intricate devices, fleur-de-lis, coronets, crossed arms and banners. Illuminations like those held captive in the minarets blazed in its eye sockets with an unexplainably inverted light that sucked the mages' brilliance from the sky and concentrated it into the embroidery of its coverings.

The man walking beside the unicorn appeared to be armored, though Aden thought that he was, instead, naked and the polished metal surface only his skin. Baroque swirlings of men and improbable creatures covered him. As the unicorn and the man walked across the plaza, drawing their light from the air around them, the interaction between the figures on their dress became apparent. Ships and dragons set out from the mountain-bound harbors upon flame-colored seas and ventured from the man's greaves, upward along his thigh and torso, and then leapt onto the swarming heraldry of the unicorn's caparison, instantly compressed into two dimensions and idealized into gold and silver monotones on the blue field. Barbaric hunting parties descended along the man's cuirass, pursuing chimeras with diamonds for each of their twenty eyes, onto the unicorn's saddle and then, with sudden dignity and abstraction, along its crinet and chanfron like engravings in the metal, until they all disappeared with the mages' light into the creature's eyes.

The day's parade of wizards was comprehensible within the meaning of the City, but the unicorn and its attendant occupied another order of perception. Aden thought them to be among the most beautiful things he had ever seen. The sight of them drained his fear away for a moment, as they had the sky's light; perhaps this was why Donchak had fallen as he had. "Where is it going?"

Donchak pointed to the domed building.

"On its master's business?" Although the unicorn was moving diagonally across the square, and therefore away from them, Aden found it increasingly difficult to speak.

"To pray."

Aden's eye glanced at the other man and found that Donchak was inexplicably growing calmer. Blood pressure and heart rates dropping, skin conductance dropping, muscle tension relaxing. "To whom?" he asked, somewhat bewildered, for is not a servant to render allegiance to his master alone?

"To god."

"Which one?"

Donchak smiled with the functional part of his mouth. "Why, to its own, of course." He faced Aden with the sky illuminating the left half of his face, making him look almost normal. "Neither magic nor science has any real claim to theology, yet. Only the Office really concerned itself with that. I would have thought you knew that." Then, moving his head away from Aden to face the unicorn, showing his rutted, slagged right side: "But I have been away from the world for years now and have no idea how far our efforts at understanding have taken us." Blood pressure and heart rate increased a bit. "No. Not in that direction or else there would have been tanks in this square months ago and the jets would have shot down all the gryphons. Wouldn't they?"

Aden thought the man was speaking mostly to himself and so divided his attention between Donchak's unconscious physiological signs and the unicorn. The truth of the immediate situation, he felt sure, lay somewhere between the two.

"We will leave your modification with the unicorn." Pulse and heart continuing to accelerate. Donchak crouched low and then pushed off into the square.

The fountain in the plaza's center commemorated some protobattle whose specific identity changed as the brass plaques at its base were changed. Again, the counterpositions: in Aden's world the thing would stand for what it was originally built for. When the commemorated victors later became the remembered defeated, it would be torn down amid the shouts of the populace, and a new one erected. Its figures would have the features of actual men, not blank idealizations to serve as the templates for the identities of the mob. Faces, names, dates, crests and arms would have been set and locked solidly within historical experience.

Here the fountain was purely allegory, infinitely flexible and adaptive to a world shared by more than one dominant race.

The unicorn and its attendant passed behind the fountain. Donchak, an indefinite shaft of red and yellow in the infrared, shifted and dodged, keeping the fountain between him and the two creatures. He did not move so badly for one of his age and weight; still, he nearly fell once or twice. Aden felt the beauty of the unicorn being edged aside by his own returning fear and distrust of the City's world.

He waited until Donchak reached the fountain and then followed, running carefully, avoiding the random spells and anomalies that Donchak's eye had not been able to pick up. His own eye showed him how exposed they were. With the magicians practicing their abilities, the only things absent were the limited wavelengths of visible daylight. Great floodings of every other form of radiant energy showered down from the sky or from the towers and minarets of the City's palaces and temples. Strange shadows radiated outward from him as he half ran toward the fountain, each one outlining a different presence.

He was breathing heavily when he joined Donchak. "All right, just keep behind me and get ready to make the transfer when I tell you." Donchak's voice was nearly normal again, but somehow regretful.

"Here?"

"No. In the cathedral." The selective blindess of his eye understood Aden's expression. "It is the only possibility, when it is in prayer, in communion."

"Just who do they serve?" Aden cut in, frightened by something that evaporated before he could capture it.

"A man of great power. I told you. We have to make the transfer then if you want it at all."

"Will we have another chance?"

"Not with the unicorn. There are many other places, static things like reliquaries, memorials, perhaps those heroic figures

21

there"—pointing up to the battling mermen and dolphins. "But none of them would be as close to the men of power as that one. None of them would be mobile or able to report on so many, an infinity . . ." Donchak became momentarily lost in his own words and their meanings.

"Nor would any of them be so easily detected." Aden rushed to keep the talk going. "If we're going to put this on, *in* that servant, how can it avoid knowing what's going on? It's not just going to prance around here, looking over its master's shoulder and turn all his secrets over to us."

"It will not understand, so it will not know," Donchak answered hazily. "Some pain, disorientation, especially when the block transmission signals go out, but to its conception of things, very little else will seem amiss. Anyway, it is continually under attack from its master's current enemies and being reinforced by its master's momentary allies. The suppression of its natural eye and the addition of your own will be lost in the usual input to its senses and emotions." Donchak raised his hand again, this time past the fountain and up to the zenith. "You see those jagged streaks of long-wave radiation?" Aden obediently shifted the filters within his eye; the waves were deep lavender, edged with ruby, though they might have been close to blue for Donchak's less sophisticated eye. "An attack from outside the City. That bar, transiting the waves above the northern skyline, there, is a defense set up by friendly princes. It is aware of all this, but cannot, by its nature, understand as we do."

While Donchak spoke, elaborating on the strategies deployed through the air above them, Aden stripped a piece of soiled embroidery from his shirt and kneaded it between his fingers. The threads softened and twined together in a putty-like ball.

Donchak finished speaking, but kept watching the sky. After some moments, the multiple spectrums detectable to Aden calmed. Saying nothing, Donchak stepped away from the fountain and began running in a curving line toward the domed building. The unicorn and its attendant were gone.

He judged the time and pressed the putty against his left eye. The hydrophilic plastic absorbed the anesthetic quickly. Within a minute his vision dimmed away from the most remote spectrums, then from those nearer to the electromagnetic until only visible light remained; then nothing. Sensory and analytic input ended at the same time. Cued by molecular keys, microscopic transmission links shut themselves off and withdrew into protected sockets.

He felt instantly crippled. Though he had practiced this many times, he had not thought the loss would be so absolute and that the suddenly limited world should press upon him so closely. It was as if the air had thickened around him, compressing him into the two dimensions his loss of depth perception left to him, blinding, gagging, muffling and blunting his mind. This was approximately what was truly happening, but the Office's surgeries and psychological training prevented him from fully understanding it; the Office had determined that irrational terror was preferable to the effects of complete understanding in circumstances such as these.

He started running, staying low to the pavement as he had before. But this time his steps were clumsy and he continually misjudged the distance he had to move his feet. Lines and ridges of magic, now hidden to him, brushed against his legs like insect wings, repulsive in their lush, invisible softness.

There was a huge echoing in his mind, which he thought to be like carrier-wave static, interrupted by the thudding of his heart and the sound of his breath. This was not what he wanted. It could not be what he and the Special Office had worked for.

The frozen balls of helium inside his ribs came to a stop. Their magnetic fields cut out and the motion of his running smashed them against the walls of their cylinders, turning them to colorless dust. The wire net buried in his skull and the lines grafted into his neck and torso went dead too, leaving cold tracks that he thought he could feel.

He had no idea how far it was to the cathedral's steps. He climbed them and stumbled into the shadows of the columned portico. Donchak whispered to him from the dark, and Aden's fear almost overwhelmed him. "This should be simple. You have prepared?" Aden nodded and pointed to his eye; if its circuits had shut down, the only traces Donchak would be picking up would be from the retention links holding it in place. "Good. Then you are, yourself, useless now. Follow me and keep as quiet as you can. Just follow. If you become lost in the dark, stay where you are and wait for me to find you."

Aden grunted affirmatively, not trusting his voice. He was used to examining those around him, knowing their precise reactions to specific words, tones and gestures. Such information had benefited him greatly in the taverns and brothels of the enemy's land; it had also saved him from the inquiries of the civil government and the mages' spies on numerous occasions. Now Donchak was closed to him, as the creatures inside would be.

But the man seemed to be functioning properly. He had obviously planned and anticipated Aden's arrival and the most effective way to expedite his mission. That was why the Office had sent him in years ago, long before it had any idea that a man like Aden would be sent later, or perhaps even what his task might be.

Donchak's actual loyalties, however, were becoming academic. As he had pointed out to him, the wizards knew they were being picked apart, deciphered, understood, their arts reduced to formulae easily duplicated and subverted by ordinary men and machines. They were getting scared, underneath their silk and velvet trappings, and some people at Lake Gilbert had seen panic infecting their habitual illogic. The risk of carrying the eye, even with its nearly undetectable energy leaks, therefore increased daily, and became almost suicidal during the monthly block transmissions of compressed data. Soon, the wizards must begin looking carefully at their world and they would see him as clearly as the eye had seen them. It had to be discarded and the orders were to leave it in a place where it could continue gathering information.

Possibly, Donchak had had similar instructions for whatever might have been placed in his right eye socket before Thorn River and the Border Command snatched it away from him.

The main doors were made of brass, engraved with the same complex designs that were set in the alabaster windows above them. Donchak nudged Aden away from the columns and led him through a small door to their left.

Aden blinked his right eye to adjust to the interior. Spheres of were-light hovered distantly in the nave, turning the marble floors to dusted silver but failing to give any indication of where the building's roof might be. Aden found himself straining to define the building's distances and colors; all his remaining eye allowed him were gray lights and pools of impenetrable shadow.

Most churches are built with many subtle distortions and trompe l'oeils concealed within the alignments of their masses. The idea is to deceive the worshiper's sense of perspective and to make the building as much a part of his devotions as the words of the liturgy—or at least to make him feel as if he is in a grander place than he really is. Assuming such tricks were present here and that the building was not under the spell of one or another of the men of power, the unicorn and its attendant were about one hundred meters away, in the center of the nave, twenty meters before the main altar.

Donchak led him down the northern aisle, the nave's supporting columns screening them from the unicorn. To his left Aden noticed various recessed chapels and crypts. Occasionally the drifting were-light illuminated one, but the contents remained closed to his comprehension.

The attendant was kneeling, his head resting against his chest, hands hanging straight down along his sides. The unicorn stood patiently behind him. Neither showed any sign of life. The figures on the unicorn's caparison had melted into a spider web pattern that hid its contours like fog. The figures on the man-creature's skin remained distinct but were frozen in attitudes suggestive of prayer.

Everywhere, everything was silver-gray with only the ivory and cinnamon of the high lancet windows to relieve it. They stepped through this hazed atmosphere like swimmers, moving with great care so as not to cause eddies in the air around them, vortices that might brush against the unicorn and its attendant, intrude upon its devotions and alert it.

Donchak stopped behind a column and watched. Aden knew it was possible that Donchak was seeing the physical reality of what held the creatures so transfixed. He might also have come here to pray.

He pressed his thumb and little finger against each end of his left eye socket, and brought them together gently. The optic nerve and the muscles that manipulated the eye were already severed. It compressed noticeably and he felt the last retention links breaking under the pressure.

The eye fell out into his other hand. He thought: There I am, my third and twentieth dimensions, my ability to see and understand, reduce, particularize, analyze. For a moment he expected the rest of his limbs to begin dropping onto the floor until he was nothing but a heap of individual components. That was how the computers at his home knew him; was it not, therefore, reasonable to think that that was how he truly was?

But there was a feeling of relief that he did not fully admit to himself. He was unsure if he wanted to see what the eye could show him in this most powerful and disturbing of places. He could turn his own eye away from the chapels, but, if the Office's eye thought it necessary, he knew that it could see through his closed eyelid.

Aden touched Donchak on the shoulder and held the eye out to him. Donchak took it, weighing it in his hand and doing little to conceal his distaste.

Donchak edged around the column and out into the nave. He grew smaller to Aden's remaining eye, but seemed to get no further away.

Aden again felt the designed terror and grandeur of the cathedral. Deprived of the eye, he could no longer reduce light or motion to their component parts or analyze the transmutation of physical substances into etherealizations by covert spectrometry. For a moment, Aden thought himself to be sinking to one knee, but found he was still standing, pressed against damp limestone. Balls of were-light dipped and wandered about him, patrolling the length of the nave. Infrequently, one would venture between the columns, illuminate one of the chapels and then return.

With great effort, he focused his attention on Donchak. The latter was walking obliquely toward the unicorn. Aden hoped the other man's sandals made no sound, but the rush of his own, unmonitored blood made hearing tricky and deceptive. He imagined groups of the lights to be clustering above Donchak, following him across the nave, spotlighting him for whoever else might be worshiping or was worshiped in the chapels.

But these were surely random gatherings. As soon as he had one formation clarified, it would slowly shift and scatter. Anyway, if Donchak was being watched, the patterns of the lights' watching would be those of high magic and not rationally perceptible. They could only be suspected and felt, never diagramed.

Donchak was alongside the unicorn now. The top of its jeweled saddle was level with his head. Donchak seemed to be moving his lips and speaking inaudibly to the creature. If it heard, it gave no sign.

The man-creature remained immobile, his posture frozen into an expression of remote listening. Aden's mind roared within itself for more information, more lines, more colors, more movement, more known factors and dimensions. He had not even been able to see the attendant's face. He did not know if the attendant had one. Nor did he know whether man and unicorn were slave and master, equals or perhaps the component parts of a single being. All he could perceive in the metallic light was the robed fat man moving as carefully as a mountaineer along the flanks of the unicorn, his hands suspended over its caparison and chanfron.

So suddenly as to make Aden nearly gasp from surprise, Donchak spun upon his right foot and stepped squarely in front of the unicorn. Its horn appeared to be made of twisted strands of gold and ebony and was over a meter long. Donchak stared up at it for a moment, as if he were examining the design on one of his blind weavers' looms. His back was to the attendant, but he did not seem to care. His lips kept moving, and Aden heard certain unidentifiable words.

Donchak twitched and shifted with a multitude of small, painfully circumscribed gestures and muttered phrases. Bloated and maimed as Aden found him, he managed to imply that some feat of enormous physical and spiritual strength was being performed, as if he had made himself some kind of fulcrum for the balancing of violently opposed forces. Aden knew that if he was right in this feeling, that he and the unicorn, its attendant, the cathedral itself, the two eyes of the Office and uncountable other forces were part of the balancing. He could not immediately decide whether he was more frightened by the fact that Donchak might be able to do such a thing, or by what the consequences might be if he failed.

His right hand describing intricate traceries, Donchak carefully reached inside the shield that protected the unicorn's right eye. He held himself like that, perched on his toes, his legs visibly shaking from the effort.

Then he brought his hand down and walked backward alongside the animal. He followed his original path across the nave, reentering the aisle several meters from Aden. He did not wait there, but continued to the door.

Aden watched the unicorn and the attendant. They were precisely as they had found them, frozen, perfect, lost in the contemplation of their own terrible infinity. Then he imagined that Donchak had left him there and rushed after the man as quickly as his fear and blindness would permit. The alternating avenues of silver light between the columns played across his eye, distorting and confusing his sense of distance so that he almost tripped and fell over non-existent obstacles several times.

There were noises behind him. Scrapes and shufflings that could have been the unicorn and the attendant rousing themselves, or the echo of his own breathing trapped by irrational forces in the chapels and crypts on his right.

Donchak was waiting for him at the door. He shoved Aden through with startling strength, but then checked himself long enough to close it with no sound louder than that of the tumblers in its lock.

He was cradling his right hand in his left, and his blasted features flowed without interruption into his functioning half, poisoning it by its pain alone. Aden dug into his pocket and offered him the remainder of the anesthetic. Donchak accepted it and rubbed the substance into the palm of his right hand, and then outward on his fingers.

When he had finished, he walked down from the portico. Instead of directly crossing the square, he turned south and entered the first side street. The road narrowed quickly. The houses became more dilapidated and the smell worsened in proportion to the distance they traveled.

Aden nearly walked on the other man's heels out of fear of becoming lost. Inside his new blindness he knew that his threats of exposure had been a terrible thing, but if Donchak had meant to dispose of him and thereby protect himself, he would have done it on the way to the cathedral, not after he had left the eye with the unicorn. But that, he reconsidered, might have been the whole point of it, to trick him into giving up the eye . . . The Office could have foreseen these variables, made allowance for them, given him reliable contacts and firm alternatives for action. But that was not the Office's way.

The mage-fires glistened over them. Now that Aden could see only within a narrow range of the electromagnetic spectrum, he thought that they had dimmed somewhat. Paradoxically, he felt more awed by them; he could not see and isolate the heavy particle bombardments that were directly affecting the workings of his cortex, producing the feeling.

"Are they still there?" he finally whispered, after the streets had begun to twist toward where the City's docks had been.

Donchak shrugged and looked to the sky. "Possibly. Perhaps there were no wars or assassinations or upheavals desired by their master tonight. Or perhaps he had a particularly terrible act in mind and they are still gathering their courage and powers for it." He spoke more to the paving stones than to Aden. "They are strange things. At times I wish . . ." He broke off as they passed by a party of lepers butchering the inexplicable smoking corpse of a dray horse.

"What did you do? My eye . . . ?"

"The eye is with the unicorn." Donchak turned down another, still filthier street. The houses soared above them, leaning together so closely that in spots their gables and balconies touched, cutting the sky down to irregular slits of auroral brightness. "They go there every night to pray. I do not think even their master knows fully why. They are totally creations of magic, more completely than any other thing in this part of the world, even more than the beings the magicians have created out of pure thoughts. They are weapons, healers, vessels of great power and vulnerability. They are very old. Some say they were alive before the War itself." Donchak's voice grew tired and he stopped to rest against a wall.

He resumed walking after a minute, picking up another street. They were probably circling back toward Donchak's shop, but there was no way to be sure. "I simply made sure that they were both oblivious to us and then placed the eye into the socket of the unicorn. I hope I was correct in assuming the Office was still using K-type connectors?"

"N. Very little difference, but much more reliable." Aden felt himself regain some control over his feelings; shop talk does it every time.

"Then the thing will function by itself."

"Yes, fully. But I still can't imagine how you did it. The thing had its own eyes. It just wouldn't stand there with its groom or companion a few meters away and let you mangle it." Aden had meant to say more, but he remembered how easily the eye had lived inside of him for the past few years.

"I understand both of them. Not their purpose, I admit. I have no wish to do that. But I do understand their presence and the way they define themselves to you and me and to their master and to each other." Aden thought that he had heard the refugees coming back from Thorn River using the same tone of voice that Donchak was. It was a sort of chanting, internalized, polished and given to an artificial syntax which only emphasized the speaker's bewilderment with the things he was explaining. "The unicorn and the man are things of purest magic. The eye is a thing of irreducible logic. It exists in the same place as the unicorn's true eye. The two are hardly aware of each other's existence. Each one reports the things that it was designed to see, in the language suited to those perceptions. The creature should feel or detect no more than a remote irritation. It just does not have the capability to understand or guess at what we have done and neither does its companion."

"But we do." A hint of condescension.

Donchak exhaled lightly and it might have been a laugh. "Not entirely, not perfectly. For all I know, we might have made a trade and the essence of the unicorn's eye is now coexistent with mine, and the picture of your face is hovering before some gentlemen of power."

Fear crossed Aden's face. With his grid, Donchak could see the deepening flush and the sparking of loose connectors inside his left eye socket, like a brooch or pendant. "Could the unicorn ever learn to see with it? I mean, apart from whether it works for us or the enemy uncovers it?"

"Impossible." The Thorn River voice again, but more slowly as if the possibility hadn't occurred to him until Aden mentioned it. "No. I think we have the advantage in this. If the eye was like the devices I remember, you could not have scratched its capabilities in less than a decade. It could be addictive, you know. Such a perfect analytic tool as that could come to control you. One keeps looking, forever looking and discovering, peeling back layer after layer of apparent truth until one begins to wonder if the layers are infinite or whether, weighing it all in your hand, you have not felt its mass fractionally diminished, and know that you possess a device that, with patience, will reduce it to nothing."

"Could, will that happen to the unicorn?" Aden was wondering just what the Office had given away, and why.

"No. I told you that. The two, the unicorn and the eye are mutually exclusive. Interaction is impossible." Donchak might have sounded irritated, but Aden could not tell; he had forgotten how to read faces with his own eye. "Anyway, you are rid of the eye and, I presume, the main object of your mission. You should thank me, Aden. I have saved you from some agony."

"The war demands a great deal from all of us," Aden responded, hoping to say the correct thing and guessing that he had not.

Donchak turned the blank side of his face to him, saying nothing more until they reached his house.

"Will you stay?"

"You have asked me that. In any event, I doubt that the men of power would let me leave."

"Are you that closely watched? They apparently didn't know what we were doing last night." Aden sipped the tea Donchak had warmed.

"They watch me in the manner of their world, as I elude them in the manner of my own. I only wonder if I can survive myself in all of this."

He could not stop some of the tea from drooling down the right side of his mouth. "I have many things here. Friends, though all secular and powerless, a prosperous trade, the sympathy of some ladies for my face and for my blindness. If I were to go back, I fear that the desire for complete understanding would overtake me again. I understand enough."

"But you refuse to understand any less. You understand so much of this City, Donchak. The unicorn and its attendant. There's nothing back home that can begin to guess at them." Despite what he had just done, Aden found himself becoming irritated with Donchak again. *The fellow speaks as much nonsense as everyone in this place.* The locked doors and shuttered windows allowed Aden enough room to think that way.

"It is a question of perspective. At this moment, I feel up against some kind of limit. I have seen and taken apart all the things I can. I can feel the edge of my abilities here because to go beyond them would require a kind of seeing which I am not capable of.

"But, at our home, I remember things having been different. We were still beginning when I left. We had been looking for only a century or two, but we were aimed for . . ." Donchak's slagged features hardened. "We had only been looking for a century or two before we could see things like Thorn River. See ourselves seeing it, dissecting and analyzing ourselves as much as the magicians.

"They only look at themselves, you know. And did you know how repulsed they are by us? How sickened?"

"It's their fear." Aden replied.

"That as much as their pity and disgust." Donchak's voice was as it had been when he first mentioned his hatred for the Border Command and reluctance to help them. His condescension and unctuous sympathy frightened Aden as much as it had the first time; it seemed to be founded upon an elusive base of contradictory vision that not all the Office's deft equivocations could equal. "They see us as thieves and desperados, intent on destroying everything of any beauty or life."

"What beauty has their war been fought to keep safe? They declared it, fought the first battle at the Burn, murdered their first town there."

"The beauty they are fighting is their own," Donchak said with even malice. "They know it. They will protect and keep it safe from everything."

"From the eye, too?" Aden used his best point and exhaled with the effort of its saying.

It worked with more visible impact than had his threats of exposure. The conversation was fixed on treasons and betrayals, Aden thought, and was it not therefore proper to remind Donchak of his own most recent one? "That was done for you and the Office. The information—if there is any that can be understood by you—must be kept apart and guarded. The unicorn has access . . ." his voice trailed away in its own sudden weakness.

"I'm sure they know, but I'll tell them again when I get back." There was some genuine feeling to Aden's words, and he was surprised by this.

"Then for that alone, and for them"—he gestured to the dimly luminous spy entities—"you should go. In the morning you should go." Donchak started to walk away from him when his expression shifted again. It was so slight that Aden could not be sure if it was not his imagination, which was only now coming back under his control. The eye, he told himself bitterly, the eye would have seen it, and the electrical and fluid currents that had flowed beneath his skin through nerves and vessels torn apart by the enemy at Thorn River and imperfectly repaired by his enemies at home. Or perhaps it could not. Donchak, Aden was becoming more and more aware, while not a total traitor or adherent of magic, was something of an alien, a foreign creature whose lunar features and moods did not function according to the dynamics of his home world.

"You should not, I think, go the way you came."

"What?" Aden could not remember saying anything about his route to the Holy City.

"You should not return the same way. Things, clues, hints of what you were might still be lingering in those places, though they might not have been traceable to you here. They can still read your mind, you know, if they want to badly enough."

The idea struck Aden as amusing: rather like trying to read a book with all its pages torn out. "Then how? Air pickup would be impossible even if there were some way of notifying the Office I needed it."

Donchak's voice shifted as subtly as his expression, with such indefinition that Aden missed some of the words as he tried to confirm or dispel his suspicions. "No need for anything so daring. I would only suggest that a more cautious and relaxed route be used." He walked around the room, idly tracing the designs in his rugs with his burned fingers, sometimes gesturing so that it seemed he was caressing the waverings in the air that Aden guessed were the spy entities. "Go north from here, through the Fishers' Door, to the City at . . ." He spoke a name that escaped Aden, saw the man's ignorance and used its old name: Clairendon. "The ocean is still there, and if it has continued to please the men of power who hold sway there, there will also be a river. Follow it inland." Donchak went on describing landmarks and reference points that Aden only half paid any attention to. He thought the general outlines were clear enough, however, and found that his conception of the route Donchak was suggesting fit his recollection of the central kingdoms. After some time he thought he had matched enough foreign place names with remembered aerial photographs and radar composites to be fairly sure of the way.

He was intensely tired, and that might have been part of his mood too. The trip would take much longer, but the prudence of Donchak's suggestion could not be ignored. Now that the eye was gone he could easily miss traps set by his enemies or by his own inattention. The way it had been, as he reconsidered it when Donchak had left him in a second-floor storeroom, was almost easy; trying it a second time, in reverse and half blind, would probably be much more difficult. He recalled crossing the square to the fountain, and then the part when he had run from there to the cathedral without the eye.

The rugs on which he lay were hard and stiff with newness; the blind weavers' designs framed him in Donchak's darkness, and he wondered if they were ones with magic woven into them. He wondered if they were floating in the air; the room was without windows and there was no way to tell if he was not, or if the magic was of another sort.

He studied the dark around him again and found nothing. But the Office, whatever its intentions, would surely give him another eye when he returned, and that would permit him to understand.

"Wake up! Wake up! They know! You must leave!"

Aden bolted awake. His right eye was filled with the bright rectangle of the door and Donchak's face centered in the middle of it. "You must go! Now!" There was nothing in his left eye but the coolness of morning air. He felt that he had awakened inside a narrow pipe. The previous night and the memory of who he was came back with painful slowness while Donchak was holding him and shaking madly.

He tried to read Donchak's face. He saw no temperature or conductance differentials, infrared differences, muscle movements or nerve signals; the man's back was to the lighted door and he could not even simply see his expression.

The panic came without any knowledge. That had not happened for years and he was sickened by his own lack of control. He tried to stand, fell from his new, unarticulated fright at the knowledge Donchak's "they" had stolen from him in his sleep, then rose again.

"Here." Donchak shoved a wadded bundle of clothing into his hand. Another man came into the room, took him by the shoulders and propelled him out into the hallway. It was lit by animal fat lamps and stank as the City's alleys had.

Aden pulled on his shirt as they half ran along it. They turned, entered a stairwell that was lit by a single panel of stained glass that ran the height of the building; the pattern was of a golden serpent and the sun behind it burned into Aden's eye, dispersing the bits of rational thought he had managed to arrange in the hall.

"They know, they know!" Donchak kept repeating with monotonous panic.

They reached the ground floor. Donchak grasped his hand once, and the other, silent man took him out through the same back gate they had used the night before.

The sun was unbearable for a moment, though at that hour in the morning the alley was still screened by the houses on the other side. Aden choked on his own helplessness, and therefore let himself be guided down the reeking alley and out into the turquoise streets. He thought that they were heading in the opposite direction from that the temple had been in, but that was of no consequence.

The streets became wider and more populated. Food sellers' and spice merchants' stalls flashed by along the limit of his vision. Aristocratic ladies escorted by parties of elaborately armored men walked among them, sampling the newest delights in jewelry from the South, carved furniture from the East, the skulls of centuries-dead admirals just recovered from the bottom of the City's exiled sea and set with gemstones, gold and tourmaline for those among the City's powerful who were inclined to the unusual and ironic.

The man beside him remained silent, guiding his steps with a strong and certain hand on his elbow or shoulder that always seemed to be intended to keep him slightly off balance. Aden considered trying to escape, but doubted if he could break the larger man's grasp; if he was trained, he would sense the tensing of Aden's muscles in preparation for any violent movements. And even if he did escape, he would be lost and a prisoner of the City itself instead of Donchak's man.

The City's life swirled around them. Grand houses, palaces, temples and government buildings rose on either side of the street. Their gates were guarded by animated statues that challenged some who came too close, welcomed others or simply watched with their enormous gemstone eyes. Aden shrank away whenever his stare met them. His eye had shown him that some did emit some kind of rudimentary power, while in others the effect was purely psychological. It was impossible to tell the difference now and the weight of their presences fell over and against him with disturbing substance.

This is what they see, this is what they feel, every day of their lives, he thought to himself.

There was shouting ahead and the man drew him from out of the road and alongside the wall of a garden. They stopped and waited as the noise grew louder; like his vision, Aden felt that his sense of hearing had become flat and two-dimensional, with the depth taken from it. The difficulty in breathing which he had experienced in the cathedral came back to him, although the sun was now fully into the sky and ordinary people thronged around him.

The party broke through the crowd to his right. There were two magicians, ten mounted deaths and four dragons without riders. In the cathedral the newness of his blindness had helped dilute the sight of the unicorn and its attendant as much as it had accentuated their unworldly beauty. He had had some hours now to remember how he had been before the eye was implanted and to think and reflect upon how he had become even less.

37

He could not tell whether they were great men of power returning from their work or if they were of lesser state, going to attend their masters and to learn the lessons of the night's battles, for they both wore masks of beaten silver. So perfectly idealized were the faces on them that Aden was momentarily convinced that his own features had been placed on them. Then he found the courage to blink his eye and the masks returned to gods or demons, depending on how the light struck them.

The crowd's babble grew as the magicians approached, and then stopped abruptly; comparative silence encircled the party at a radius of twenty meters. They came within five meters of where they stood and Aden heard the pounding of his heart explode into the quiet that enveloped their passage.

Dust rose from beneath the hooves of their mounts, but Aden could see it only as gold. The ten deaths, more gorgeously attired than those he had seen the day before, trotted with agonizing slowness behind the magicians, at a speed calculated to allow enough of their stench to reach the crowd and give proof of their immortal decay. Strange and frightening devices, suggestive of the price the magicians had extracted from them for their release from their graves, spangled their tunics.

That was all there was, suggestion, hints, outlines drawn with nighttime darkness in the morning, extending backward through all the perspectives which the loss of the eye had denied to him. Aden felt the mystery of the City as its people did and cowered before it. Yet he could not look away.

The dragons strode behind the deaths, hazed with the golden dust, moving at a half-march with their long, reptilian legs, the natural armor of their chitinous hides indistinguishable from the light camails and segmented breastplates their masters had given them. Their eyes shone with internal light and revealed a murderous intellect.

They paid no attention to him and passed. Evidently they were not privy to the knowledge Donchak was. The noise struck up again, as it had the day before; the ritual of that hour ended.

Beggars rushed away from the wall and into the street, scraping at the chinks between the paving stones where the magicians'

dust had settled. Aden looked down and saw their fingers beginning to bleed before they were knocked over by the renewed
progress of more sober-minded persons.

The man grunted and resumed walking. Aden felt his fear
replaced by shame and then by the morning's confusion. His
sense of personal abandonment became impenetrable and he did
not notice when Donchak's man had to get him out of the way
of another passing man of power as his palanquin was borne
across their path by eight cyclopes.

The Fishers' Door had been erected where the canneries had
been in the old city of Cape St. Vincent, when there had been
such things as oceans, and before there was any need or thought
of walls for the City or doors carved from fused bodies of the
wizards' vanquished enemies.

Aden passed through the Door and stared dully up at the thousands upon thousands of forms, faces contorted in agonies that
might be still continuing; arms, limbs, hands, all intertwined
around each other and frozen into the two huge slabs of the
Door. Their endless features were blurred and remote, as if a
layer of smoked glass held them together instead of the power of
the City's wizards, but Aden's remaining eye could still see
enough to be sickened. As with the two magicians, though, he
could not look away. The brutality of the Door was too mon-
strous for him to encompass, and even with the eye, he suspected
that the motives for it might have escaped him. Again, he was
left with the mystery and found it quite enough.

The man abruptly released him into the currents of men and
beasts that compressed themselves into the Fishers' Door as they
entered the City or left it, spreading out onto the branching,
marble-paved roads that led out to all the other kingdoms of
magic. He had said nothing, shared none of Aden's confusion
or Donchak's apparent panic. Aden wondered if the man even
had a face, for he was able to remember only blank, dark skin,
outlined with traceries of purple tattoos. He also recalled the
attendant of the unicorn, who had also been faceless, yet as warm
with lives and patterns. Perhaps, he hypothesized as the crowds

swept him past the Door's thousands of tormented eyes, it was the function of such blind and faceless men to guide creatures like unicorns and secret police spies before the former had gained their eyes and after the latter had had theirs taken from them.

The City's walls soared above him, their height impossible to estimate with his single eye, covered with murals and mosaics that raced away from him into blurred, violent luminescence. The Door's traffic carried him away from the City and pushed him off to the side of the road. The land around the walls was gently rolling prairie and the light colored it the same gold and bronze that the light in Donchak's house had been; Aden saw that it did not reach into the Fishers' Door and the eyes there shone with light the magicians had put there, and none other.

"They" knew. Donchak had said so. But the mission was mostly completed, with rather more success than his superiors had probably anticipated at its beginning. The wisdom of Donchak's suggested route still seemed correct, despite the way the man chose to make sure he took it. Imaginary alarms might have been sounding in the City. He thought that he could hear the deep tolling of bells above the roaring of the road's traffic.

He walked for most of that day. Once he learned to compensate for the false distances his eye conveyed to him, the miles passed with comparative ease.

There were few magicians abroad, for there was little need for them to resort to mere walking or riding where long distances were concerned. The road was a wearisome place for them, and perhaps evocative of restlessness and questing, and therefore to be left to ordinary folk and commerce. The familiar tiredness of the road and the harmless pageantry of its traffic replaced his fear. The memory of Donchak's faceless servant vanished first, for there seemed so little to the man. Then Donchak fell into some kind of perspective of his own, that of a simple traitor or harmless lunatic.

The unicorn remained, however, dimly attended by the metallic giant, floating alternately through the darkness of the cathedral's nave and then through the new emptiness of his eye socket, waiting in both places for the summons of their master, carrying the Office's treason with it to spy on his designs and plottings.

People spoke to him, reassuring in their trivialities. Strangers remarked upon nothing more sinister than the beauty of the weather or the fields of wildflowers that the road gradually climbed into as it left the City. Drunken centaurs yelled and screeched to themselves as they pulled cargos of women to the City's markets. Despite the obvious poverty of his dress, men still approached him to peddle ornaments and charms of indifferent workmanship. There were also other fellows who cautiously approached him and offered articles that could not be purchased where the magicians were closely watching: prisms, rusted ball bearings, charred printed circuits picked up on centuries-old battlefields. The road was more open than the City, even though he often saw rocs patrolling the skies above it.

Following Donchak's directions, largely because he had no others, he continued on the road as it went north. It became less grand as it left the immediate territories of the Holy City, losing its marble paving blocks and turning to cobblestones and then to packed dirt, but the people on it became no less fascinating. If anything, Aden marveled at how easily they had fitted their mortality around the presence of magic. Palaces rose distantly through forests of sapphire-oak and diamond vine, or perched on fairy tale escarpments too eccentric to permit any real menace to flourish. The formations of rocs diminished until only solitary eagles with wings of translucent carnelian watched the road for the magicians. Magic was always in evidence, but usually as ornament or backdrop. Women wore necklaces of were-light and occasional seers had wildly grotesque familiars perched on their shoulders, but there was never the hint or implication that forces of illimitable power were being kept and refined, or that vengeances were being harbored against entire nations and philosophies.

Aden wondered if it had been like this on the roads he had

taken on his way to the Holy City. He could remember nothing on them but brutality and oppression by omnipresent powers. Even when the magicians or their retainers or tentacles of power had not been detectable to the eye, he recalled a different spirit in the people. He could not believe that the loss of the eye, great though it may have been, could have changed his perceptions this much. Donchak's suppressed rage at the Border Command or his ostensible panic were different, more complicated things. Here he sought only to know if a person was smiling or walked with his weight on the balls of his feet so that he could move suddenly to this direction or that. Surely he did not need the eye to understand such things.

Perhaps it was simply that the hold of the City or its belligerent sisters was not so strong in these places. Or, he thought again on the next day, perhaps this was just a sign that the war was ending. The reasons became less important as the beauty of the countryside increased.

Clairendon seemed a reversed image of the Holy City, where the constructions of magic underlay those of the old world, rather than the other way around. It had once been a port and it remained one despite the magicians' dislike of the ocean, anciently the highway for his world's battle cruisers and submarines. Its clapboard houses were intact as were its open, wandering lanes, the palaces of the mighty hidden among them as discreetly as they had been in the forest. Its men of power did not seem to have the morbidity of taste that their brothers in the other cities of magic did; they could be seen tacking through the harbors of the city in magnificently carved pinnaces, the visible display of their power limited to the filling of their sails when they moved against the wind.

He spent more time there than he had intended. Its magic, like that of the road, was made of soft, intensely human stuff, even when it was wielded by immortals. Its sky glowed only fitfully at night, and then as much from the auroras as from the battling of the magicians.

But the season was progressing. It was already midsummer and he guessed there would be at least one stretch of high country to traverse before he could reach his own lines. He took the road that bordered the river flowing into the ocean near the city, as Donchak had suggested, climbing back into the emerald and turquoise forests and their singular peace.

The first attack came one week after he had left the ocean city. The road followed the river in a gently curving arc to the west and southwest.

At first Aden was pleased that his remaining eye was sharp enough to see them approaching up the river valley, utterly silent because of their speed. They seemed like motes of dust, anchored in a gently shifting space that did not quite match up with the one the river and the road occupied.

Their size also grew according to different laws of perspective than the river's. They were small for an overly long time and then their dimensions exploded outward, instantly growing wings and vertical stabilizers, gun pods and iron bombs slung from hard points, aerials, turrets, blisters and canopies, their proportions suddenly gigantic.

Aden thought his heart to be stopped; but he had perceived all of their approach in the space between its beating. They were bombers and the alternating black and red stripes on their wings showed that they were from the fortress at Dance. The span of their wings bridged half the river's width. Their leading edges and noses were glowing yellow from the speed of their flight.

The people on the road looked up calmly, wrenching their shoulders and necks to keep the aircraft in sight, and then looked back to their fellows or to the oxen they were leading. No one but Aden showed any surprise. Fearing discovery, he forced himself to stay on his feet and keep walking.

The sound of the ships and the blast from their weapons hit him simultaneously, knocking him to his knees and compressing all the air from his chest.

Two men dressed in turbans and satin robes grasped him by the shoulders and helped him to his feet. "Are you all right?" the shorter of the two inquired mildly.

Astonished, Aden turned to face the man. His features were long and finely drawn despite his lack of height. A column of thick smoke was rising from the river shore directly behind his head. "Just a surprise. I didn't . . ." Aden wondered dimly if he was using the correct accent.

"Of course. The land around here is so enchanting. It is so easy to forget about the War." His voice was patronizing but Aden detected no suspicion in it. The two men then stepped back, bowed slightly and merged into the crowd. Aden followed in their direction, edging toward the river's shore.

He found a shaded spit of land and walked out onto it. The strain of trying to appear unconcerned made his limbs move in jerks and he felt that all the magicians' spies were now watching while their masters decided whether it would be worth their while to crush him.

Nothing happened. He turned his head downriver. The line of smoke reached up far above the bordering ridge line of the river's valley. But it shifted and bobbed uncertainly as the aircraft had, subtly out of phase with the world around it. Aden saw a large river trireme at its base and guessed that it had been the planes' target. It was untouched, suspended within the smoke like the eyes of the vanquished people in the Fishers' Door, its oars moving with their own slow rhythm. People moved nonchalantly about its decks; the water around the ship was smooth, broken only by its wake.

Aden watched the smoke thin away and disperse. The trireme stayed, moving downstream. Its flags and rigging remained motionless, the crew and passengers showing no more acknowledgment that anything unusual had happened than the people on the road.

On his way to the Holy City, he had seen occasional evidence of his world's assaults on this one, but he knew that these were usually ancient freaks, when the laws of probability had allowed the destructions of his world's weapons to coincide with the constructions of magic's. He had never seen one of the futile attacks before this, and he thought he felt a careless, languid triumph in the people on the road. The ships had come, raging with their geometric fires, and done no more than cast a shadow across the sun.

Aden got up and back onto the road. The feeling of invincibility grew stronger, reaching into him and sparking something that might have been contempt for the futility of the way his world was fighting this war. Midday fireworks, but little else. He found it equally difficult to understand what Donchak had so feared about the implantation of the eye. It had been there for over two months, yet even the ships from Dance could do nothing.

The second attack was an artillery barrage directed at a palace made of malachite. Aden knew that he was still at least six hundred kilometers from contested border areas, so it must have been rocket-boosted shells launched from diminishing caliber Gulrich guns. Aden spoke the words to himself and marveled at how out of place they sounded.

They poured down from the stratosphere into a tight circle around the castle, wrapping its towers and turrets in spheres of gold and scarlet fire. The barrage lasted for half an hour, and Aden watched all of it from a grove of dwarf pines by the side of the road.

Whenever there was a break in the shells, he saw the castle's emerald beauty inside the fires, inviolate, too indifferent for contempt, its flags and pennants rippling lightly in the winds of this world alone. Large hawks and gryphons from the castle occasionally rose through the detonations, containing their explosive ferocity with the simple grace of their flight.

There was the light and the vision of destruction, as there had been on the river, consuming themselves without reference to their intended targets. But this time, there was also a singing inside his mind and wild, incoherent bursts of electric shrieking coming from the places where the Office's annunciators were buried.

Aden thought that it might be evidence of the gunfire reaching out into their target world, touching it with more certainty than the smoke column's shadow. Again, the people on the road reassured him; they turned to observe the attack, or stopped and chatted with their neighbors against the backdrop of the explosions, but then moved on showing no more interest than they had for the attack at the river.

The sounds came in step with the explosions. Aden recalled as much as he could of his own circuitries, tracing their patterns under his skin as if he were reading a map of a newly alien country. If it was not the Office, calling and asking him to range in the distant batteries, then it might be the detonations themselves.

The eye could have seen the lines of electromagnetic force whipping outward from the inviolate castle, prodding sympathetic currents by induction from the wires and dead, metallic masses. He was still of his own world; he could see and hear the violence of its war, however futile the kingdoms of magic rendered it, and he was again surprised at how saddened this made him.

The shelling stopped. Aden got back to his feet and stepped back onto the road. His ideas of balance and accommodation remained consciously intact, but he felt the reasons for them dissolving before the invulnerable beauty of the castle and the countryside. The power of his world was becoming as shrill and panicked as he had imagined the wizards of the Holy City to be.

Emerald light engulfed the people in front of him. He watched as they jerked themselves around to stare directly at and then through him. His heart folded in upon itself and he was momentarily convinced that he had shown his guilt too clearly. But they were looking past him.

He turned also, and found that the southern half of the castle was gone, replaced by a dense cone of green light. He glanced back to the road and saw the teamsters and merchants squinting silently at the new light; their faces were suddenly as unreadable as those in the Holy City had been when he had first lost the eye.

Aden pushed himself into the standing crowd, excusing himself quietly in the deafening silence, moving as carefully as he could around their gaze. "They have found us," a man muttered as he passed; his voice was not upset, but the words were there. Aden thought within himself that he was the man's and the castle's "they," just as the man might have been one of the "they" Donchak had warned him of. He turned involuntarily and found that the man was looking in his general direction and that his face was covered by a mask of woven gold with faceted, obsidian eyes.

"Only this once," a companion said, and Aden thought that the man had raised his voice just enough to permit him to hear it. The second man's face was also covered, this time with a smooth chromium mask whose eyes were closed and whose mouth was locked shut.

Aden slowed and almost replied to the two men. But he found that the only words in his mouth were embarrassed assurances that the explosion had been an accident, just the odds playing that had characterized most of the war's centuries. He said nothing, but the men adjusted their blank and closed eyes to stare pointedly at him.

Aden knew that it was early fall, but it appeared as if the magicians of this area, however discreet their palaces and ways, favored spring and summer. The road left the river and climbed steeply into highland plateaus; snow-edged mountain ridges could be seen on either horizon, but he found the meadows full of blooming wildflowers. The groves of ghost pine were speckled with their white and turquoise cones; in Aden's world, they produced such cones only once every five springtimes.

The land had been but recently conquered by magic, and many of its cities and villages were still half ruin. Glowing hulks too far away to tell whether they were of rocs or gutted half-tracks spotted the mountainsides at night. Aden found the effect not as sinister as he recalled it to have been in the lands in front of Joust Mountain or around Castle Kent and Everwhen, where such wreckage had been allowed to remain as memorials to what had happened there.

He left the road and climbed up into the alpine meadows to examine one of these memorials, vaguely thinking that, if it proved to be a device of his own world, he should be somehow obligated to discover what he could about it, so that the descendants of its crew would know.

Halfway there, he saw that the light had been reflected by a white pavilion whose fanciful tangle of columns and ornamental beams resembled a roc's skeleton from the road. A garden spread out from the structure, lighting up the mountain with long splashes of brilliant color. Rose vines and morning glory, still in flower though it was afternoon, climbed up and through the structure, ornamenting it as gorgeously as any of the gold-encrusted temples that the lowland kingdoms had erected to their patron deities. Streams of silver water ran down past him, and he crossed over them on footbridges of rock crystal.

Aden recognized the magic in the place, but by now found himself able to enjoy it. The destruction of the castle had been largely forgotten; the small victory of his world had been buried in tens of other futile attacks on the road or upon the cities it linked together. He had watched, first in fear and in shame after the castle's destruction, then with greater calm as the rockets or shells curved down from space, imperfectly guided by satellites which, after twenty years of probing, had still not found an immovably fixed point in the kingdoms of magic on which to fix their ranging lasers. Inevitably, they missed, falling into streams or groves of flame-willows that smothered the violence of their detonations.

The fighter-bombers were always the same. They bobbed and wavered through the air as the first ones he had seen did, their crews probably sick and disoriented with the way the world outside their windscreens or radarscopes refused to conform to what they sensed were the motions of their ships through it.

Aden found a clarity of vision in the fires that they left. As they burned themselves out, seldom touching anything, they acted as a lens for the beauty and strength of his enemy.

Before, the eye had disassembled, and explained the world in rigorously comprehensible forms. The fires acted in the same way. He watched the world's beauty, sometimes inverted or split apart in simulation of a prism, its components arranged and recombined, not according to any final scheme of priorities or energy potentials, but according to the way they were formed by the men of power. He watched them growing through the explosions of his own world, saw the individual brushstrokes of their creators expand apart, suggest their genesis in the loves and triumphs of other mages. He believed that he could feel a great substance and weight of emotion underlaying the creations of magic, entirely separate from the realities that his world assigned to them in the parallel spectrums.

He briefly wished for one of his world's attacks, but then reconsidered that the fragility of the pavilion's grace needed no explanation or analysis.

There was a chair in the center of the pavilion. Aden stopped and turned around, looking for someone who might occupy it. He saw the two men several hundred meters away, in the direction of the road, one with the chrome death mask and the one with the black stone eyes. They stood apart from the traffic of the road, staring in the direction of the garden with their undirected gaze.

They were as they had been when they observed the destruction of the emerald castle. In memory, he also found their opaque faces in the crowds that watched the attack on the river trireme; and after the castle, during a rocket barrage that fell upon an astrological observatory that had spread outward four kilometers on either side of the road, and when squadrons of dive bombers from the fortress at Whitebreak had emerged from the sun and squandered their fury on the ice gardens that some magician had carved from his personal winter.

Donchak's "they"; possibly, but he could read as much serenity and mystery into their masks as he could menace and pursuit. They seemed primarily watchers, as was he.

There was enough, however, to dry his mouth and accelerate his heart perceptibly. He turned away from them. The chair in the center of the pavilion was now occupied by a figure in pale blue robes, with a loose cap of darker material.

He had previously avoided any approach to persons of obvious power, but this one appeared relatively mortal. The person was only seated amongst magical works and not clearly magical herself.

Aden began walking again. If the men from the road were following him, it was unlikely that he could do anything to throw them off now. He also found the presence of the woman in the pavilion resolving itself into terms he could understand. First, he had seen only the beauty, without immediately assigning any gender to it. Then, like the beauty of this world seen through the lens of the other's obsessive destruction, he recognized her as something human and impenetrably mysterious, composed of parts that could be seen, detected, yet never quantified.

The whores of this world had been decipherable to the Office's eye as biological and elementary mental functions; at times the eye had hinted to him that he had seen their souls. The eye of his own world, having been trained and selectively fed and starved on the Office's peculiar diet of perceptions, had seen less clearly, but had nevertheless understood enough. This was different; at last his eye had come upon a new way of seeing on its own.

Her hands were flawless. She was over fifty meters away, and he saw that clearly. The nails were closely trimmed and her fingers were long and had almost no creases between them.

She was holding a book. As she shut it and looked up to him, he saw, first, that its cover was of light tan leather into which many designs and emblems had been patiently worked.

The bone structure of her face was precisely drawn beneath pale skin, but her nose was smaller than most and her eyes correspondingly larger. She might have tended toward the sterile idealization that the mask of the man on the road had, or those of the two magicians who had so terrified him when he was leaving the Holy City; but instead of stepping over this line to inhuman abstraction, her beauty veered slightly before its own mirror. Enough reality remained to reach into his own world; she instantly summarized all the racial perfections he had seen in the kingdoms of magic by being, ultimately, unlike any of them.

"Aden?" she said over the distance that remained between them. He did not think it at all remarkable that she knew his name.

He nodded and smiled up to her, wishing for something to cover the emptiness of his eye socket. He was in rags, his beard was tangled and he smelled.

Her eyes were gold and olive, but shifted into gray and then back into a turquoise as he tried to decipher them. She brushed a strand of auburn hair from her face and he saw a spark of blue light, dancing at the end of one of her fingers like a miniature star freshly picked from the night.

"Is this yours?" he said when he thought himself close enough to be heard; he was delighted that his voice came out with some clarity and strength.

"Yes. This and most of the mountain behind it."

Aden felt the enemy's world rushing away behind him, and he involuntarily looked around to check his own position in it. The road was still below him, choked with riotous pageants, but the two men who had been watching him were gone.

Surprisingly, she was still in the pavilion when he turned back. "You seem to know my name. What's yours?" The war twisted and heaved distantly within his mind; it coursed up and down the limits of his cranial net, trying to prod more echoes from the attacks he had witnessed from the road. Not even Donchak had known his real name; only the Office's eye had known.

"Gedwyn."

"Are you part of the war?" the wires and dead annunciators inside of him asked transparently.

She laughed as if he had said something amusing, and put down her book. "No more than you are. Have you come to take all my secrets from me?"

Aden pointed to his eye. "I'm afraid such things are a little beyond me right now. I . . ."

Her features saddened, and Aden was instantly embarrassed that the suggestion of his blindness should have made her feel that way. The fact that she had known the secret of his name but not of his wound occurred only to his crippled parts, his wires and semiconductors; they strained against the unaccustomed warmth and peace that they sensed around them.

51

The garden was attacked four days after Aden had arrived. Gedwyn had left him for the morning to watch, she told him brightly, for the different sorts of peace that she could see traveling along the road. Aden nearly pointed out that he had seen very little peace on the strategic maps at Castle Kent. But he did not want to risk her displeasure, and was not sure he had ever seen such maps in the first place.

Surely, she had the power of transmutation. Aden therefore lay on his back, staring up through the ghost pines and wondering if any of the hawks or pegasuses he saw circling above him could be her. He wondered if it had felt this way seven hundred years ago—before the war came and crushed all but some of us. The war, he had often read, had swept away all the dreams, as all wars had the habit of doing. But Heisner had demonstrated that the way this one was being fought would not only prevent their returning with the peace that might be won, but would destroy them along with their enemy.

Instead, he saw the cruise missiles gliding along the ridge lines, dipping and shifting clumsily with the rough mountain updrafts. There were four of them in a diamond formation, holding tightly to one another so their ECM boxes and radars could protect them from the pegasuses.

They banked to the right and drifted down the slopes toward where he was. Aden got up after a moment. The intrusion of his world registered slowly at first. Then their geometricity cut against his mind and he felt enraged that they had presumed to disturb the peace of Gedwyn.

"Aden." She was at the end of a path, terraced on either side with banks of orchids.

He opened his mouth to warn her, but could not define the peril to her.

The first one struck a kilometer behind her, where the pavilion might have been. The shock wave blew the folds of her dress forward in the direction she was walking; her hair was also lifted like a nimbus, diffusing the following light of the explosion around her face and turning the paleness of her skin to gold.

The two flanking missiles struck down on either side of the path. Their concussions pressed her clothes back against her body, dissolving the violent abstraction that the first had given her.

The inside of his head roared to him, but Aden found the noise remote and hardly noticeable. Aden saw the fireballs thin away as they ballooned outward from their impact points, until they were only veils of yellow white when they reached her.

Small bits of litter, individual leaves on trumpet vines burst into sharp flame, like the one that Gedwyn wore on her right hand. They, like the veils of fire from the three explosions, wrapped themselves around her, as the were-light had around the unicorn and its attendant. Aden marveled at how easily the anamorphosis of this world transformed the structured violence of his own into its serenity. He watched with his single eye, seemingly able to detect the individual molecules that chose to give themselves over to the missile's combustions, and those that remained as they were. The abilities of the Office's eye diminished in comparison to the perceptions of his own, and he briefly wondered if the Office's wires and antennas were listening and watching what he now saw.

The fourth missile struck against a waterfall in the grove behind him. His cranial net screeched as the outer currents of its explosion reached him. He was not Gedwyn nor was he made of the garden's magic. More flowers ignited on the ground as he fell toward it, his personal blackness obscuring her, but allowing him to see the look of concern that crossed her features. Aden, in turn, felt ashamed that his death should in any way cause her displeasure.

The missiles had been hunting their enemies in dimensions other than those which Aden or Gedwyn or her garden occupied. Aside from some burns on his back and a persistent ringing that hovered about his cranial net, Aden suffered no serious damage.

The star on Gedwyn's hand, however, was gone. She said nothing about it, but he associated its extinguishment with a dark shading to her voice. He found her awake at night beside him, holding her hand up against the night sky, the orbits of the Office's imagined satellites tracing across the sky behind it. His eye could see a thin line of scar tissue running along the finger that the star had been on; its texture was rough, but it reflected the silver of the sky and the glowing cones of the ghost pines with a gentle parody of what had been there. His one eye saw that even her wounds were made of enchantment.

She did not. With the passage of days, the uncertainty that he had discovered in her voice grew deeper. She spoke, instead of his own secrets, of her concern for the safety of the garden.

She was an immortal and had planted the garden during the first, great flowering of magic, before the triumph of rationalism and the discovery of light and empiricism. She and the garden, like many of the creatures of power, had gone into hiding in those centuries that followed.

She had emerged when the alignments of the universes shifted to summon them back. Before the cruise missiles had found the garden, she had held bitterness and unbelief only for the fact that a war had attended their return.

Her references to the first, ancient retreat of magic increased. Aden noticed that she spent less time in the contemplation of her book, and more staring at the road or up to the sky. She fell into the habit of rubbing the scar that the four cruise missiles had inflicted upon her against her lips, perhaps talking to it and asking it where the star had gone.

Aden wondered if the star had been the intended target of the missiles. He asked Gedwyn this once, as they sat on the rim of a fountain, watching butter-colored hollicks building their miniature caves in the boles of ghost pines. She only shrugged in reply and looked again down the meadows to where the road twisted away from them, toward the border.

In contrast to what he perceived of her changing mood, he felt his enchantment for her growing to such an extent that he wondered if she might not be using her powers to do more than simply pry an occasional secret from his mind. But this seemed both unlikely and presumptuous. He was, he constantly reminded himself, but a fraction of her real age and an agent of the nations that had sent the missiles against her.

The second attack came when winter had closed in around all of the mountains but the garden. The snow line reached down to the road and the people on it were dressed in fabulously dyed furs that gave them the appearance of hollicks from the distance of the pavilion.

The garden kept its summer. The water from its streams and fountains ran freely and then froze into crystal glass mounds where it crossed out into the countryside. The tracks of hollicks and chamois led to and from the garden through the surrounding perimeter of snow and ice. The nighttime air had the same clarity and sharpness that he remembered it to have had in his home. But he could lie naked in the garden's evening beside Gedwyn, seeing her hand sweep across the galaxies, and wonder what he might possibly have brought to the garden, aside from the missiles and his own dead circuitries, that could have caused her to let him stay. He had never had the occasion or asking such questions at his home.

No warning this time. The sky simply turned white, as if a light had been turned on in a small room.

The wave fronts reached his cranial net and shouted a warning before the light was fully perceptible. Still, he almost opened his eye, as if he thought he could see what was happening and tell Gedwyn that a fusion bomb had been set off at the top of the atmosphere, and that by the time he had finished telling this one thing to her the snow would have been melted from the valley and the travelers on the road for a hundred kilometers would be charred husks within their furs.

But she placed her hand over his eye, protecting it, he imagined, with the finger and its scar; he thought there was a sense to this, the wounds of his own world protecting them both from later, more terrible ones.

55

He felt warmth beating against his body, casting web-patterns of shadow along the shallow ridges of buried wires, revealing the few trivial secrets that he had managed to keep from Gedwyn. This lasted for a minute, and then ended.

She took her hand away. There was a lavender blur of light centered in his field of vision, but that was all. The garden was intact; the hollicks picked up their quiet night conversations with the nesting rocs and pegasuses.

"That was ours," he said unnecessarily; the wizards' combat had never been so quick or monochromatic.

"Do you know what it was?"

He told her, and then: "But, like the missiles, it doesn't seem to have been meant for us. Not even a near miss this time." Aden stretched himself on the summer grass, feeling its contrast to the sharpness of the stars.

Gedwyn sat up and then rose to her feet, like someone whom intruders had wakened from a half-sleep. "That was the garden, I'm afraid"—addressed as much to the hollicks as to Aden. The animal sounds fell and then stopped.

She put on a cloak and padded carefully away from him. Aden got to his feet and followed, again embarrassed at the clumsy barbarities of his world and at his own uneasiness with being left alone in the quiet.

Low flower beds opened onto the meadows, now clear of snow. The length of the road seemed to be on fire and its thin guttering line was suspended in a featureless, smoking dark. The quiet of the world outside the garden was absolute, and Aden's cranial net reminded him of the "dead rooms" the regular services kept at Lake Gilbert, where every sound and echo was absorbed by fiber cones and the men who were being tested in them were suspended in chicken wire cages in their centers.

Gedwyn drew her breath in sharply, and continued like that, as if she were breathing through a gag of coarse fabric. She held her left hand out before her; the scar on her finger picked up the light of the burning road as it had the winter stars. Aden could sense her trembling. He wanted desperately to comfort her, but he felt all her endless centuries of grace and power beside him, facing his blind eye socket, visible only in two dimensions, and that only if he turned his face away from the valley.

The road kept burning. In areas that he thought might have been those she was pointing at, the fire seemed to flatten out and verge toward cooler, more metallic colors. But it flared back to its original intensity as soon as she moved.

He thought that he could hear snatches of foreign languages between her sharp inhalations. For the first time in months he was reminded of the nighttime streets of the Holy City and the pathetically majestic battles that were always being fought over them.

Gedwyn stepped away from him, seating herself on the pavilion's throne and continuing her mumblings and gestures. Shoals of winter air drifted past his skin. Processional instabilities could be felt at the edges of the garden's interface with the new, burning winter that his world had brought.

It, they had "known" of this part of the world, Aden slowly realized, his heart shriveling with sickness and shame. Information that had not been available before had become known; they had deciphered it and explained it to the bombs they sent out. This one had understood, more completely than the fighters on the river, or the artillery shells or the cruise missiles.

He wished for the eye. Gedwyn's mystery was enough, so long as it was her own; now the bomb had posed one that surrounded it. While it could not touch her, it destroyed everything that surrounded her wonder, isolated it and left it spinning in its own dark patch of existence. Its knowledge placed Gedwyn into a crushingly reduced perspective, and, with it, Aden's feelings for her.

He had last felt this exposed when he had fled the Holy City; after that the road had hidden him from everyone but the two men. Now he stepped away from Gedwyn, conceiving against his will that whatever he felt for her had been treacherously lured out from behind the Office's defenses. The two men did not need to watch him any more for his presence would be easily perceptible to any magician who cared to look, even if Gedwyn did not.

The bomb had seen him, the satellites must have, the side-looking radars of the planes that constantly traced the borders between science and magic had seen. He was part of their war again. Gedwyn's withdrawal, if such it was, meant nothing. She was still tied in all her beauty and gentleness to the war, as much as the eye and the cruise missiles were.

Aden felt his nakedness and how the burning winter dark brushed against it. He turned and walked into the garden. Gedwyn was still standing in the pavilion, moving her hands in disconnected arcs. Aden wondered whether she was trying to reassert the authority of magic over the valley, or simply trying to keep the garden's summer intact.

Aden walked toward the center of the garden, seeking whatever warmth magic's laws of thermodynamics had concentrated there. He became aware that he was being propelled as much by his own confusions as by any desire for immediate safety or revulsion with the bomb's casual incineration of the valley.

The war was back inside of him. Unconfirmable lines of force tying the bomb's spent power to that of Gedwyn, and Gedwyn to Donchak and the Holy City, and Aden to all of them proposed themselves. The wires inside his skull stayed silent, but their matrices provided convenient frameworks for his speculations to attach themselves to and replicate.

Heisner's mythologized fear stood beside his shame, both watching his mind begin to shake itself apart. Gedwyn was becoming lost in her own bewilderment and in the brutal shroud of perception that the remembrance of the war infected Aden with.

He was running. His clothes were piled under some laurel trees, a hundred meters from the pavilion. Aden scooped them up and pulled them on clumsily, without losing much speed except when he got his boots on and laced. More hypotheses came to him, unbidden. The possibility that what he felt for Gedwyn was love was more disturbing than if she had simply enchanted him as she so obviously could; the spells would be her own and, like her other mysteries, unknown to him. But Heisner had dissected love and found only two pages of calculations. Aden was no mathematician, but imagined scraps of equations intruded into his mind, coolly chipping away at Gedwyn's image, invalidating and falsifying what he felt for her.

All the fragile, humanly scaled relationships that he had discovered since leaving the Holy City frayed and came apart. The forces and threats that they had held in equipoise strained abruptly at the limitations that they imposed; they spun wildly at the ends of the tethers of Gedwyn's beauty, the garden, the gentle chaos of the road and of Clairendon.

Against this and his own self-disgust, the overpowering logic and perception of the bomb was comforting. It, in contrast to everything he had touched since he had reached the Holy City, met Donchak and yielded up his eye, was made of immovable things. It had spoken in a single voice whose one meaning carried across every part of the parallel spectrums that it chose to address.

The valley's winter instantly stripped away the artificial warmth of the garden. He fell on the ice that edged it and hit solidly on his right side. His hands skidded across the rough surfaces as he levered himself up and plunged into the snow. That also was only a border. The ground beyond it was still warm from the bomb.

He continued running downhill. The cold air stank of burning flesh and all the cargoes that had been traveling the road twenty minutes before. His feet moved erratically in the mud. The guttering line of the road grew before him, deadening his night vision so that, even when he did look back, he could not see where the pavilion was. He ran along its edge, an uninterrupted tangle of intertwined caravans, wagons, corpses, blurring into long smears of color on his left. Eventually he was able to generate enough pain so that he did not think about Gedwyn or try to decide whether the dreams to which she was so irrevocably tied were worth that much sorrow, or, if they were, whether it was because he had nearly made them his own.

The bomb's summer deceived the flowers and trees that the magicians had scattered along the length of the road, triggering profusions of stunted blossoms that contrasted uneasily with the black and brown wreckage.

That lasted for five days. Then the bomb's presence faded and the valley's winter came back in a single night, freezing all their colors and snapping off new stems like glass. Aden emerged from the blasted caravan in which he had spent the night and saw the borders of the road marked by trees that were half in bloom and half in winter, like cheap china figurines. The wind was enough to break them, and all day, as he walked, he heard this sound like a fire, inhabiting the frozen mud and tangled corpses.

The weather did, however, reduce the smell.

The road ended ten days after he left the garden at a walled city whose minarets were all jagged, broken stumps. From there, other roads led back to the east, or to the south or north, but they all curved away from the west, where the alpine plain sloped downward toward a pink-and-salmon-colored wilderness.

Aden searched through the city for a day and concluded only that it had been deserted for some time. There was fresh water and he managed to trap a roebuck who had broken a leg trying to escape from a complex of empty alchemic laboratories.

The altitude dropped quickly. The patches of frostbite on his feet and hands healed and scarred over as the weather improved. The country, also, became scarred and barren. It was crisscrossed with rills and dry riverbeds that slowed his progress. But the land protected him from thinking of Gedwyn; its clean brutality drew lines of distance and memory between her and his mind.

The comings and goings of aircraft increased. Their contrails served the same function as the riverbeds, drawing lines all around the world, quantifying it according to their inflexible wisdom. Gedwyn became lost inside of their limitations. She was again the enemy sorceress and he, again, the escaping spy.

The first evidence of his own world was a mound of slagged and rusted metal. Sections of gears and I beams protruded from it. Aden could not guess what it had been. Aden guessed it to have been left over from the very first engagements that magic had fought with science. From here, the wreckage should get progressively more recent, like the geologic ages of the fossils pressed into the stratified sandstone cliffs that he passed under.

Instead, one hundred meters from the wreck, Aden found a sentry tripod. It consisted of three braced legs, a central column which housed its perceptors and a laser ring; two blue and orange beacons were stacked on top. The whole mechanism was made out of machined stainless steel.

The sand had blown up around the base plates on its legs so it must have been there for some time. Magic had not moved against the tripod but allowed it to stay and watch, serving as a base point for the triangulations drawn by the surveillance planes and cruise missiles.

The man was dressed in a khaki walking suit with a wide-brimmed hat against the world's sun. He was sitting on a shooting stick and looked quite at ease despite the two wrecked bombers on the lake bed behind him. "They've been like that for about eight years now. Experimental stores, you know. Pity they hadn't been dropped on our friends over there." He got up and pointed at the hulks with his stick. "Havinga." The man went up to Aden and shook his hand; his skin was rough and cool and tanned a shade darker than his clothes.

"Are you from Dance?" It was the first Border fortress that came to mind; his lips were cracked and it hurt to talk.

"Only the Office. We've seen you coming for some time. We, ah, picked up a trace when you left the eye and Donchak turned you in, and then later . . ."

"Donchak?" Aden found the man's memory distant enough to question who he had been.

"Ah, yes. Really nothing we could do about that. You were just too far in and the only thing we still had planted on the old fellow were perceptors in that eye. I don't think he has any idea he's still a little wired to us." Havinga had a large, open face and the sort of coarse features that a tan looked good on. Aden liked the man immediately, despite what he was telling him. Donchak was another age and place. His profession had been treason and betrayal and he could not find any reason to reproach him for it. "Of course we got a clear fix on you in that garden, but the Border Command had other ideas by then. I really can't tell you how sorry we are about that." The Office knew of Gedwyn, as it had of Donchak, and he quickly changed the subject. "But, you know, the war's been going rather well lately—that eye of yours has helped us enormously—and it may be that we're finally getting ourselves out of a job. Have to recall even old Donchak and pension him off."

Aden felt himself suppressing laughter at the absurdity of the conversation. Havinga must have seen this, for he smiled more broadly and clapped him on the back. Aden almost collapsed but kept on chuckling, louder and louder. "My eye?"

"You can't believe how friendly the Border people have been to us since we let them have some of it. But don't worry, only enough to let them win their war, nothing much else."

Enough to find the garden and the valley? Aden was laughing too hard to ask.

"Certainly wish we could plant one of those eyes on the appropriation committee at Castle Kent, though."

Havinga took him by the elbow and led him away from the burning airplanes, toward an open car parked beside a grove of blood-colored thorn trees. The dry lake bed dropped away behind it to the horizon, where Aden thought he could make out green hills, topped with the magic whiteness of his world's Border fortresses.

Etridge was nearly old, and he thought: They are dying. The scopes and visual readout arrays in front of him reflected the idea on three-dimensional graphs. Above him, the aerials interrogated the mages' world. At regular intervals, silence engulfed the world and they listened to it in bunkers a hundred meters below the nickel-steel roofs. Then the active ranging units would cut in and their energies blasted across the land, probing at the shrinking frontiers of magic, raining down tropospheric and stratospheric scatterings, or battering horizontally against them, streaming through the passes and valleys of the Cameron Hills.

For months the reflected energies had shown them less and less. The static and carrier waves had come back to Joust Mountain unmarked for twenty-one consecutive days. The recordings were restudied and reanalyzed, because the traces were undoubtedly there; the skies above the sacred cities had to be glowing, the secrets of the wizards could not have been completely unraveled.

After seven hundred years there was quiet. The people at Joust Mountain, and at the other Border fortresses of Dance, Whitebreak and First Valley hypothesized progressively more subtle stratagems and deceits of the vanished enemy. Perhaps, instead of leaving, the enemy had only set them back to where they had started through one stupendous feat of magic, so enormous and pervasive as to have its limits drawn beyond the range of their instruments. Perhaps, then, all the green-and-yellow-bound notebooks of computer and special group analysis were now invalid, the universe upon which they were premised and toward whose understanding they had pointed discarded and irrelevant to the future centuries of the war.

Because of this and his age, Etridge also felt anger and frustration. They could not be permitted so easy and conclusive a victory; they chose this universe as their battleground and they had no *right* to move to another. Neither could they die, he raged inside his tightly locked heart; we have worked too hard to understand everything about them.

"Well, where are they? Where?" He was aware of how clearly his irritation showed.

"That, I should think, is your job." The man from Lake Gilbert was the same age as Etridge, but since he had not spent his years at places like Joust Mountain, his voice contained only bewilderment and a shading of relief. The enemy had vanished. That was enough. If it continued that way for a thousand more years without a single new fact being uncovered about them, he would be satisfied.

"Are you sure the regular services haven't taken any offensive actions—commando raids, plagues, new sorts of bombs, missiles, anything we might not know about that might have thrown a scare into them?"

"Your rating is higher than mine. The services have left that part of the war to the Border Command. We only move against the enemy when he appears inside our lines. And then we always give you people a chance to look them over before we try to cancel them."

Eighty-three thousand people had died under the mages' basilisks or been turned into blocks of fire, while reconnaissance drones instead of attack ships overflew the slaughter at Thorn River. Etridge had helped supervise that observation. He had watched his scopes as he did now, and seen the thousands of deaths individually translated into quanta of light, energy, plasma, and magnetic disassociations. He remained convinced of the correctness of what he had ordered there and was bitterly defensive at any hint of its being questioned.

"If there had been anything like that, you would have known."

Etridge was glaring at him, pale olive eyes clear for his age, focused on a point within the other's skull. The man from Lake Gilbert self-consciously edged away; he felt as uncomfortable with Etridge as he did with everything else at Joust Mountain. He told himself that this was wrong. Etridge had often proved himself a fine and courageous man, and the fortress itself had been the place of his world's first blind victory against the men of power. The lake that had separated it from the Cameron Hills had been destroyed in that battle, drained and evaporated by the forces that had contended above its surface. Its bed was a featureless plain, seeded with the wreckages of hovercraft and dragons. After five hundred years fragments of the dragons' animating power remained, turning their skeletons from ivory to obsidian to shell, twitching and shifting, gradually working themselves down into the dust.

Etridge had ordered a study of their disintegration as contrasted to that of the aircraft and tank hulls. They found the decay was more orderly in the latter case; the steel and aluminum proceeded through various forms of oxidation, or else their radioactive fuels decayed through their half-lives, pacing through the periodic table with planetary certainty, their paths described by straight and predictable paths that always ended in known, stable elements.

The variables which controlled the dragons' rot took much longer to understand. Before that had been achieved, Etridge liked to think that the servants of each culture retained their masters' perspectives of the universe after death. The decay of machines was mechanical; the decay of the dragons was, like their life, pure mystery. But in the act of discovering the mechanisms of the dragons, he came to believe that he had converted them to his conception of the world, that he had reached across the lines to grasp their peculiar and individual deaths and summarize each one in the notebooks held prisoner in the fortress. Ultimately, he discovered an allegiance of their deaths to the life of his world.

He could do this because Joust Mountain was also where the first inquisitory antennas and computer banks had been installed, one hundred and ten years before Heisner's suicide. As the world's mania for understanding deepened, it became surrounded by whirling dish antennas, and the walls and revetments protecting its guns were buried under latticed towers.

It covered a ridge five kilometers long. To the east the grass and cottonwood trees grew up against its walls. On the eastern side, where the land sloped down to where the lake had been, all obstructions had been removed to provide open fields of fire. This land was charred and crystallized into rough glass where the antennas' energies had burned and ended every living thing in front of them.

The use of such high energy levels was unavoidable. It was often the only way the enemy's secrets could be penetrated. On evenings when the passive aerials were shut down and the active ranging systems monopolized the parallel spectrums, the sky over Joust Mountain flared as it did over the Holy City when the men of power were sharpening their skills.

Now, at Etridge's recommendation, all of Joust Mountain's facilities were on line. Passive and active systems operated together by occupying alternating sections of each spectrum.

Etridge stalked along the oddly formal terraces where the turrets of siege guns had been replaced by side-looking radars. The man from Lake Gilbert, several inches shorter and more adequately fleshed, walked behind him, then dropping back and nearly becoming lost in crowds of uniformed fanatics clutching the colored notebooks that seemed to be the fortress' main currency.

The facing walls on their left were blank and slanted upward to shoulder away the concussion blasts that the magicians had never thought to use. The ceramic armor had been perfect when it had been installed, four hundred and fifty years ago, and aside from a light brown defining the seams between the plates, it remained untouched for all the thousands of meters of the eastern galleries. Except where someone had managed to scribe the words "reductio ad imperium," in careful script. The words would not have been noticeable to the man from Lake Gilbert except for the same tan discoloration, an indication of the motto's age.

"Where?"

"I said, there have been no offensive actions of any sort."

"Then they've gone. Do your people have any theories?"

"The continuum is infini . . ."

"Goddamn it is."

"Infinite, and the possibility always exists that they have opened up new areas of it." The man shrugged. "First there was one spectrum, then the parallels were discovered. Possibly there are divergent areas of existence."

"There hasn't been any action on their part for years. No appearances, no creatures of light in the streets, nothing freezing the air inside jet engines." The man from Lake Gilbert realized Etridge was hardly aware of his presence. "I wonder if we've acquired something like a critical mass of understanding. Nothing sudden, but just gradual accretions, year after year. Half the old magazines here are filled with reference books and tape summaries, all piled up, cross-indexed, cross-referenced, constantly revised and brought up to date by newer findings. Our computers talk to at least a dozen other Border installations on a reg-

ular basis. They can tap into nearly every unit of any consequence in the world if they feel they're running into a particular
problem. Could be. Just enough."

"But our knowledge alone could hardly make them vanish. Retreat and re-entrench maybe, but not just vanish." The man
wished he was back at Lake Gilbert, walking with his morning
coffee along its quiet hallways, confronted by nothing more disturbing than the portrait busts of dead heroes.

"They listen to us, you know," Etridge mentioned offhandedly. "Not in the way we examine them, disassemble them, and
do the same to the pieces that are left. They just listen now and
then in their own ways." The contempt and condescension in
Etridge's voice was unmistakable; the man from Lake Gilbert
thought it inappropriate. "We only began to understand how
they did it about eight or nine years ago. They use a number of
means, but the non-corporeal ones all operate on the same final
principles. Of course, there was no real reason to interdict them."
The man from Lake Gilbert paled at this. "Joust Mountain isn't
an offensive base, just a forward observation post that happens to
be impregnable. All their listening and watching could tell them
about was themselves." Etridge began smiling to the east. "Joust
Mountain: the Wizards' Mirror. We just kept at them, about
how they did what they were doing."

"That can't be what happened. You seem to be speaking entirely in metaphors, not hard facts."

"Metaphor was the only way we could talk about the magicians' world until the strategic shift from offense to understanding. There was no common reference or standard in their
actions. Now, maybe, we've offered them one."

"And if they've taken it?"

"Then they've done one of three things. They have become
like us. They have found another place and time which can better protect their goddamned mysteries, or they have turned their
last mysteries on themselves and died." Etridge was grinning
broadly now; the prices other people had paid at Thorn River
and at scores of other places might have been worth something
after all. We've pushed them to the edge, he thought, shown

them the short end of the pier and the fools walked off it rather than admit it ended.

"We know it's not the first, because if they became like us they'd be tossing atomics at us before we caught on and did the same to them. I also imagine they'd be pissed as hell at us for having broken up their little game."

Little game. The man from Lake Gilbert shuddered to himself. Seven hundred years of the little game where millions had been ground to pulp between two opposing forces that could not understand each other well enough to carry on the well-ordered killing of normal wars. Seven hundred years of the little game where men marveled speechlessly at the non-exclusivity of their world and the thought that other gods might stand against their own.

He must report this man to Lake Gilbert, or to the government at Castle Kent. Etridge was proposing a single, unthinkable triumph. If what he was saying was true, he should not be in a position of responsibility, not at such a critical strategic and historical juncture. The victory he hinted at smelled of Heisner's achievement.

If only there were more armed people here. He was a soldier and did not like the paradox of a frontline post like Joust Mountain being staffed with people who clung to computer readouts more passionately than the regiments at Lake Gilbert did to their automatic weapons. But then, it seemed that the people at Joust Mountain did everything more passionately than those at Lake Gilbert, Everwhen, The Corridor, Castle Kent, or in any of the cities of the world. The guns there implied respectful fear and caution; one had to be ready because one did not *know*. Know what the enemy was thinking, know how he performed his feats of wondrous violence, know when and where he might leave his preposterous castles and strike against them.

Here, they were blinded by looking into the night, against whose visitation Lake Gilbert and its divisions waited.

The man must be reported. This is not the way the services should protect their world.

"It could be that we've shown the bastards the edge," Etridge repeated. "A few more weeks, a month or two at the most, and we may have to go and look around for ourselves."

"I'll pass your evaluation of the situation along to Lake Gilbert."

The doctor, who was a machine, found Aden sitting in a wicker lounge chair. Graceful oaks and maples framed the hospital behind him. It had been the home of an immensely wealthy family before the war, and the Special Office had taken great care to preserve its Georgian tranquility. It was free of the baroque pretensions of the magic's architecture; neither did it have the sullen massiveness that their own world had necessarily adopted in the times when the enemy might appear anywhere. The Special Office had found that it greatly comforted its people.

At the far end of the lawn, where the dogwood groves started, the doctor could see the long knitting needle barrel of a Bofors gun weaving back and forth across the sky, waiting as it had for decades for the enemy, not even sure if its ammunition could harm the particular avatar he might choose. Its splayed base was overgrown with ivy that the grounds keepers had trimmed and weeded; the paint had been polished off its controls so it looked like one of the ceremonial guns that were fired to celebrate Republic Day at Castle Kent.

The Special Office thought that people were more at ease with machines that looked like machines, rather than like people. Thus the doctor, while manlike in his general form, had no face. His oval skull was brushed aluminum and it reflected the sunlight in frequencies which the Office had discovered to be comforting to its people.

The doctor walked over to Aden and introduced himself. The man looked rather older than his service record listed him to be, but that was to be expected. He sat down in another chair, slouching easily on his spring steel spine, and folded his hands in front of him.

"We think you'll be well enough to leave us in a month or

THE SIEGE OF WONDER

two." The voice, like the reflective abilities of the doctor's skin, reassured Aden. "I must say, though, that not many of us thought you'd come along so well when they brought you in."

Aden smiled to the doctor and nodded. The device was easier to talk to than an actual person at this moment. "Yes. I lost track of things . . . How long was I . . . ?"

"Less than six months after you emplaced the eye."

Aden was embarrassed by his vagueness. "So short?"

The doctor had no face but Aden had the impression that he was smiling. "Not really. You've been here for almost four more. And all of them have been rather important months, what with the war winding down and all." The doctor stretched his polished arms and looked around himself. The hospital was a beautiful place and he liked it more than any other he had been assigned to.

"I know. Donchak said that was happening in the City, and, ah . . ."

"Havinga," the doctor put in helpfully.

"Yes. He said the same thing. I wonder what it will be like, not having the war around."

"They're practicing for our new world in some of the southern districts and in the Taritan Valley. Getting wonderfully eccentric and irrelevant. Some jewelry making, art, quite a bit of music playing, storytelling and people back in bright colors. The reports are really a delight to read."

"The government's not afraid they're being subverted by magic?"

The doctor inclined his featureless head in a way that indicated amusement to Aden. "Not at all. The Border Command, of course, has its usual dark opinion of the matter, but the people at Castle Kent just feel that they're turning away from understanding and Dr. Heisner's numbers, not towards magic."

"Then it might be over."

The doctor nearly said that, yes, they'd won, but he knew the kind of victory Aden felt it would have to be. "It might." The gun was still emplaced at the bottom of the lawn and the communication aerials were still strung between the hospital's ancient chimney pots; but it might be over.

"Will we be going back if it is?"

"Not immediately. No, not for some time. Those people in the Taritan, I think, are going to set the style for the moment. People will just want to rest and get all this damned purity of oppositions out of their systems. We don't all want to end up like old Heisner, even if the Border Command thinks we should."

"And the other half of the world?"

"We'll just let it heal for a while, I suspect."

Aden looked into the soft penumbra of the doctor's face. "Heal?" he whispered, but did not know why he found the word so disturbing.

The doctor knew and he ached for the young man. "Yes. We've been hurting each other for so long. We need the time as much as the land over there will for the enchantments to die down."

"Will she be there?"

"She?"

The word came into his mind slowly and for a second he continued to look at the doctor without saying anything. "Gedwyn" —he was not sure he pronounced it right. "What about her magic? Will that be gone too?"

"The magic of her garden will go. That's where we first picked you up. You really had us concerned after you left the eye . . ."

"Then it was magic, all of it."

"Not what held you. That was, ah, love. That's why we really weren't too concerned with you and it was relatively easy to stop any treason charges from being brought by the services. They understand those things at Castle Kent more than they used to." The doctor forced himself into postures and tones of reassurance. His work with Aden had come along so beautifully, and he felt some of it eroding.

"But that is just magic too. Heisner explained that, didn't he?" Aden's voice was shaking.

"You are not a very strong man, Aden." The doctor felt it necessary to release the pressure. "Brave and honorable, but not strong."

"No. I guess not," Aden said softer than dust. The charred ribbon of the road recoiled against his heart, winding all the way from Clairendon to the sentry tripod, bringing with it the first clear memory of Gedwyn he had had since he was brought to the hospital. He wrapped his arms around his chest despite the warmth of the air.

"But, you must see, Aden, that the Office never wanted strong men. The Border Command takes all it can get and the regular services only want enough to get by. But we, you and I, cannot afford such strength. We work with too many fragile things that break so easily. But have to use them. That's been our job through these centuries."

"Who sent the bomb?"

"The device was due to be sent in anyway from First Valley. The Office just modified it a bit so that you and she would not be hurt."

"This is not hurt?"

"It's minor compared to what you both would have felt had you stayed any longer. The lives on the road were going to be lost no matter what we did. We only changed so much of it so that two of them could be prolonged a bit more." The doctor sensed Aden's acceptance of what he was saying. "Your Office continued to watch after you and after its own enemy. We only covered your treason with one of our own."

"And I could not have seen any of that by myself, without the eye?"

"You were half blind, you know. We had to provide you with enough light to get you moving again."

"I still am half blind." He touched the bandages covering his left socket.

"Yes."

"Could I have another?"

"A normal . . . ?"

"No. Like the first one the Office gave me."

There was some uneasiness in the doctor's voice, but with no facial expression to match it with Aden could not be sure. "But you know that one was a one-off project. Incredibly complex and expensive. You know it would just lead you back to where you started, back on Heisner's track. Magic is gone or at least withering. Without its mysteries to look at, you'd turn in on your own life and world.

"Anyway, the, ah, Office is being shut down. Funding has always been difficult. And now that the war is winding down, the services cannot see the need for us. Centralization, that's what they say is necessary. Things that will look at the enemy, or what's left of him, from the outside, that won't have to go there and risk getting caught when their outrage shows, or just, ah, succumbing to the appeals of that place." The machine felt embarrassed again.

Aden had not noticed; instead, he was struck by the thought that the technique of external observation and contact was just what the robot was practicing on him, as if the Office itself was distrustful and afraid of its own people and sought to deal with them from a distance.

"I just want to know why, why all or *any* part of this happened. May still be happening."

"This?"

"The war, the love, the road, Thorn River," Aden suggested for he was not entirely sure himself.

"The eye would not tell you why, only how."

"Didn't it tell the Office why?"

The doctor shifted in his chair again. His smooth oval face remained toward Aden, perceiving him in all medically and psychologically useful spectrums, vaguely comical in its pretensions at humanity. "I don't know." The voice seemed to come from somewhere else, so abrupt was the change in its tone; it was harsh and disjointed, as if it had been synthesized on the spot.

"Is that why the Office is closing?" Aden asked.

"I wouldn't know about that. Even the rumors"—the voice becoming more conspiratorial—"hardly include the eye or what it showed us. Only that it's gone blind lately." The doctor threw his outspread fingers up and away from his hand, attesting to the fraility of mere machines. "Nothing seen from it for months. Just interference patterns and static."

Aden nodded in agreement. Logically, there could be no great identity between the eye and the Office or the war. No matter how important the information received from it could have been, the eye was only a small part of each. But it had been so great a part of him; the memories of its omniscience grew, it seemed, to fill up the emptiness that he now perceived to have been left by Gedwyn.

"But it is still there, in the creature?"

"The unicorn?" The doctor replied ingenuously, "Oh, yes. At least before the carrier waves went dead. We could be fairly sure of that."

Aden thanked him and did not think at all about why a doctor should know such things.

They thanked him for his years when he left the hospital, gave him some money (apologizing that there was not more), new clothes and a service weapon.

He was empty. His left eye remained empty, covered by a leather patch; his body was still heavily woven with dead wires, empty couplings, disconnected links, empty vacuum chambers, power leads branching from his nervous system into cavities that had held the various mechanisms of the Office.

The Office and its war had been taken from him, and he could find nothing in his world to replace them. There had been the short memory of Gedwyn, but he had requested the doctors to blur this, for her remembrance had been very painful.

He therefore continued to dwell upon the Office and the war, as he had done for all the preceding years. True, the Office's war had not offered one much of the terror and exhilaration that it had provided for other people on either side. As soon as action broke out in any area, the Office always withdrew its personnel to quieter places. The battlegrounds were the conceded laboratories of the services. The Special Office preferred to watch its enemy and its powers in repose.

It had been a comparatively gentle sort of espionage, carried out by people who lived most easily in paradox, contradiction and indirection. It was predictable that the Office should have become faintly alien even to itself.

Politicians had regularly questioned which side the Special Office had really been on. The Office, not officially existing, naturally declined to respond to their accusations.

But information had been obtained, and had found its way into the computer pools of Aden's world. Most of the Office's strange, abstracted evaluations wilted under the fanatic empiricism of the services. But enough had proved valuable enough to keep the Office alive for centuries.

Indeed, as Havinga had said, one of the minor breakthroughs of the past decade had been Aden's emplacement of the eye with the unicorn. The monthly block transmissions, five-second bursts of accumulated information and observation, had for a few months provided the services with the first hints as to how the internecine battles of the men of power were fought.

But like most of the information provided by the Office, it smelled too strongly of the other world. Even before the Office was formally closed, the services and the Border Command had stopped listening to it. They had made what was judged adequate studies of the Holy City's internal politics, and reduced those studies to green-bound notebooks filled with Llwyellan Functions.

That had apparently been enough for them. Aden wondered why it had not been enough for him.

He was too old or too young to be doing this. He had not been ordered. All his commanders had been scattered, perhaps like himself, and he had known only a few of his fellow agents.

Get there, he thought. Get there and find out why he had come and then why he had left. At first he was preoccupied with just taking another step or another breath in the high country air, but that lessened in the month since he had left the fortress at

Dance. He was following approximately the same route he had taken when he had left the City. The diminishing power of the war had only slightly changed the geography.

The alpine valley was about five kilometers across with a stream traced along its northwestern edge. Sharp granite walls rose two or three hundred meters on either side, featherings of melting snow running from the ridgeline at intervals. The grass and wildflowers seemed particularly brilliant, but that might have been due as much to the clarity of the air as to the plants themselves.

His remaining eye was sharp. Although he had not fully compensated for the loss of depth perception, he could easily pick out mountain sheep grazing along fracture lines in the valley walls, a kilometer or more distant. They fed on patches of grass and scrub plants that surrounded the ruins of hermits' pavilions.

The powers of this world, like those of Aden's, had not been uniformly devoted to the prosecution of the war or in ostensible practice for it. Aden had always found some comfort and interest in the renegade mystics that were attracted to the interface between the enemy worlds. Of necessity, they avoided areas of frequent activity like Joust Mountain or the Holy City, but gravitated to areas like this. He had sometimes thought he would have liked to have done so himself, assuming a new name and holding himself out as a teacher of worldly science or a traitorous magician depending on which side a passing visitor might be fleeing from.

His feelings, he thought, must be like that the robot doctor had toward the new societies in the Taritan Valley: vague envy at the stability they had apparently found and frustration at his inability to come up with a good reason for not joining them.

He had been walking for some time before he realized that the wildflowers and long meadow grass were giving way to a neatly trimmed avenue. The wind did not touch the individual blades of this new grass, nor did it move the brittle china blossoms of rosebushes, chrysanthemums and ground orchids. The stream beds, too, became sculptured as they moved across the valley floor.

Aden slowed. He touched the gun in its shoulder holster for assurance. The pavilions he had come upon before had all been in disarray and ruin. The bodies of their occupants were bone or ash; whether they had fled from his own world or that of magic, they had apparently received a common message or come to a single conclusion. And they had left.

They had also been crazy in the first place. One could never expect too much of them and the Special Office had regarded the information they freely gave to its agents with great caution.

The northern slopes of the valley became a recognizable garden, perfect, immobile, rigidly held by a power Aden recognized as non-rational. Luxuriant creepers with lavender and white blossoms were frozen against carved rock outcroppings, hiding terribly suggestive shapes with wings and talons and crowns of fire. Small rodents were similarly paralyzed between dust-muted flower beds. The skeletons of birds were trapped in the seasonless growth. He could feel the brittle grass snapping under his boots and shattering like glass.

The pavilion was largely open, being little more than an intricate lattice of arches, columns and curling gables, and there was a magician seated on a flower-choked throne near its center.

It looked too fragile to have withstood the mountain weather, but Aden guessed that the structure and the garden around it had been sturdy enough to have stopped time, and, therefore, rain and wind should have been minor concerns.

He was satisfied with his lack of open fear. Logically, he should have stopped when he first saw the grass standing against the wind, drawn the gun, fitted the sight and let the Office's circuitries decipher their meaning. But the Office, unlike the services, had never depended totally on machines nor abdicated to their way of thinking. He told himself that he had recalled his old training, dredged it out from under his ruined heart and protective surgeries, and evaluated the situation correctly. Time was stopped here; one who was moving through time and therefore dying could be trapped only if he stopped too. That must have been what happened to the birds.

The beauty of the pavilion slowed him and invited his senses

77

into its confusing tracery. The magician inside of it was magnificently clothed, seemingly in orchid blossoms, beaten flat and overlaid on heavy gold foil. A book which he knew would be poetry, although he had never learned more than a few of the hundreds of script languages the wizards had written in, was open on his lap. The eyes were closed, yet the shadowing around them hinted powerfully at awareness. As he tried to steer to the right of the pavilion, he also noticed that its shadow contradicted the position of the sun; they were held in place by the magician's spell as absolutely as the lives of the flowers and the meadow creatures.

The immortality of the garden was that of a single moment. The magician had chosen one instant, when the relationships of all the things around him, from the line he was reading to, possibly, the specific quanta of light that was falling upon him from remote galaxies, conformed to some scheme or balance which he judged to be perfect.

It was not precisely a suicide. The uniqueness and unity of its conception slowed Aden further. He wondered where the boundary layer of the spell might be, how many angstroms above the captive flowers it hovered. The gun could understand all of it; but he found that he could not reach for it; he could only feel the anger of its mechanisms against his chest between the lengthening interval of his heartbeat.

Aden knew what was happening and part of him cursed with the gun at his stupidity and vulnerability. If he had had the eye, he would have understood all of this; the magical beauty would have been quantified and he could have protected himself against it. But it was not so completely terrible. It was like all the enchantments he had known in this world, though only those cast by the vaguely remembered love had touched him so closely.

The association eroded the surgeries and in an instant he grasped her name. Panic spread through him with the same, measured rate as had the realization of what was happening to him. He strained his eye back to the pavilion and searched through the thick, dawn shadows that covered the magician's face. Despite the hour she had apparently chosen to capture, she looked much older than he remembered. That, the doctor had mentioned to him once in a different context, was how it almost always was.

He remembered what the Office's hospital had tried to protect him from, and in the remembering slowed even more, half wishing to pass into the spell. But he could not do that. The birds had been trapped in it, but had not been chosen by Gedwyn to be part of it. So it and she held them there, transfixed by her beauty to die of exposure and thirst and starvation.

Aden felt his heart closing in around itself. He continued to look, and although the thickness of her robes completely disguised her body, he began tracing its contours, remembering its extraordinary softness and warmth, even in the artificial summer of the garden. He remembered, for the first time, how little they had spoken; but that only allowed him to believe that he could remember each of her words and the time and place she had said them. He found his body more densely inhabited by her than by the scars of the war or by the wire nets and antennas of the Office, and wished with frightful intensity that he would slip completely into the spell.

The sound of the approaching ship cut cleanly between him and Gedwyn; then it reached inside of him too, and separated him from her memory.

He was far enough to the side of the pavilion to see the approaching ship without moving his head. It was flying approximately level with the ridgeline, weaving slightly from side to side to give its cameras a better look at the terrain.

Twin-engined, propeller-driven, cautiously made of wood, though the men of power would have never condescended to look for magnetic anomalies in their routine observations; only Aden's world would have searched for intruders in such a way. Its sound deepened against the quiet of the garden and he could hear the rush of air over its wings. It traveled with a graceful deliberation that was separately visible as it diagramed its own passage through the valley; there was its awareness of itself, that included the minor ionizations and subatomic reactions triggered by its presence and by the pressures and vacuums its motion induced.

Aden felt himself moving to face it, rotating on one knee so that it seemed he might be kneeling, as he had in the temple before the unicorn. He felt the garden's power eroding in proportion to the aircraft's approach. He imagined he could feel the wide-bank cameras perceiving him, separating his being from the timelessness of the garden and only incidentally from himself.

The cold, camouflaged image of the ship, motion, and wisping oil smoke from its port engine filled his eye. Without depth perception, it came upon him suddenly, as if it moved freely through a space of its own creation; beside this idea Gedwyn's feat of stopping a single instant paled and shrank.

He saw where it had been patched from the wizards striking at it during other flights, where fins had been added or removed to perfect its movement through the air, saw the blankness of its radiation-proofed windscreen and ball turret dome.

It was a Special Office ship. It carried time with it because it believed that time could stand against magic and against the final desires of its own world.

Aden moved his head in a quickening arc as the plane flew over him and down into the valley. He found himself walking after it, past the pavilion, still looking at Gedwyn, but no longer held by her.

As he looked, a vaporous dust drifted off the flowers and the framework of the pavilion. At first he thought that it had just been the wind from the aircraft blowing free the summer's accumulated pollen. But the usual mountain wind had dislodged nothing when he approached the garden.

The haze thickened until it appeared the garden was made entirely from damp, smoldering wood.

It was the time the Office ship had brought with it, infecting the garden, gradually and unintentionally reducing its subtleties to known factors, opening up the closed surfaces that kept the air and sunlight out and Gedwyn's own life inside.

There was another sound, muffled like a hand falling on a quilt. The book had fallen from Gedwyn's lap. She, in turn, had bent slightly forward, her right hand slipping up from her chin to her mouth, shielding her hurt and sorrow. The time-mist rose from her too. The shadows over her eyes lightened as their captive darkness vaporized.

Aden started running, and his movements were sluggish and painful. Enough of his heartbeat returned to remind him of the necessity for fear. This helped. He ran through low hedges of ground orchids, kicking them into granulated diamonds.

The edge of the garden was fifteen hundred meters from the pavilion. Aden ran on for another hundred meters, feeling the freedom coming back to his legs and arms, feeling the wind again and the rough meadow grass.

He fell down next to a clump of bayonet grass, the product of the valley's first peacetime spring. The cuts it put in his right hand were shallow, and for a moment he enjoyed the certainty of their pain. Then he reached into his tunic and unclipped the gunsight from his holster. He looked back to the garden and found that the haze was gone. Everything appeared to be unitary and whole again, immune to the further progress of time.

The spell had been displaced. The book was still face down at Gedwyn's feet, and she remained bent slightly forward; her eyes were still shut but the shadows around them were qualified by an equivocal light. Every blossom that he could see had lost at least one petal.

Gedwyn still held a moment, but the ship had loosened it enough for Aden to escape. The fact that he knew the Office to have been closed over a year ago did not bother him; he had worked for it for years, firmly convinced that it did not exist in the first place. Surely, if he had lived and worked at addresses that did not exist, called telephone numbers that were not listed in any directory, talked to people whose names had been erased from all the world's records, the presence of one fugitive aircraft was hardly worth puzzling over.

But it was an Office ship. If it had been piloted by any of the services, it would have been pursuing absolute knowledges and the garden would have burst apart as the power of its spell was set free in a hostile vacuum of inflexible understanding.

In its way, this was crueler. Gedwyn persisted, but no longer in a time fully of her own choosing. Aden guessed that if any conscious thought was left to her, she would soon go mad, locked into a prison of her own building, unable to escape and correct it or choose another. The book with which she had chosen to spread her personal eternity, the particular word, faced away from her and the symmetries it had formed with the pavilion and alignments of the stars were now flawed.

He held this thought within his mind, equally with the memory of what he had felt for her. The gunsight and the aircraft stood between the two, mediating, translating, allowing him to exist with their equal truths. Aden knew that they could be removed easily and he could submit himself to the dominion of one or the other, and thus become like the Border Command or like Donchak. Such choices were not the manner of the Office; choice itself was not.

Closely packed columns of figures and symbols lined the gunsight's reticle; internal gyroscopes stabilized it against the trembling of his shoulders and hand. The gun understood the magic that remained, but Aden could not believe that it knew or understood Gedwyn, or if it did, that it could communicate its understanding to him in terms he could grasp. But the doctor had told him that the bomb had known, after the Office told it.

He dropped the gun to his side. She was again remote; her features were blurred at the distance and partially screened by the pavilion's latticework sides. She became as he was, a thing mostly of the Office's creation, and he could no longer be sure whether there was enough of the thing he had loved or of the enemy magician left in the garden to compel her destruction.

He walked away from her as he had the first time, slowly and uncertainly, scarcely daring to breathe lest the noise of the air in his lungs disturb the balance the Office had commanded and plunge him irrevocably into one side of the war or the other.

Etridge picked up the notebook Stamp had placed before him. "I didn't give you much time."

"Quite enough."

"I forgot how much things have improved now that we have fewer distractions."

"Just simple psychometric monitoring and evaluation. Interpret that with post-Heisner theorems and Llwyellan Functions."

Etridge held up his hand. "What will he do?"

"We're not that far along yet." Stamp permitted himself a smile. "But based upon what we understand about him now, he will report nothing to Lake Gilbert. The man was subjected to too many conflicting allegiances in too short a time for him to evolve a rational course of action."

"Or even an irrational course?"

"No course at all. Given his personality and the way in which he perceived things, he'll abdicate to stasis. That is safe. It's served the world fairly well for years now."

Etridge ignored the implied reference to Thorn River. "He'll abdicate to stasis and to the victory we've given him."

Stamp smiled again, but less surely than before. Now they were talking about something besides the man from Lake Gilbert. That had been a single person, like any other that had lived and like the millions the antennas had listened to, examined and probed. His background had been known and, as he told Etridge, when the understanding of his psychology and history were applied to his current experiences, his future conduct would be accurately predicted. But Etridge had placed the man, and therefore, Stamp could not help but think, those who had watched him, within the context of the *ended* war.

The war: simple, absolute, present in the sense of distant oceans or winds that seldom intruded into one's immediate life. Stamp often conceived of Joust Mountain as a university and its antennas as laboratory tools vastly removed from the phenomena they studied.

A victory would have to be claimed; positions would have to be consolidated, lingering traces of magic crushed, isolated covens rooted out, understood and ended, the lands divided and scoured clean of legend. Was that not the imperative of victories?

That it could happen this way, so quietly yet so absolutely, terrified him.

"Anything else?"

Stamp guessed that his distraction showed. "As before," he responded, shuffling the other notebooks in his hands. "Incoming bands remain almost uniformly blank. All the systems here and at Kells, Dance and other installations for two thousand kilometers report the same thing. Some traces remain in spots, and we're trying to see if they don't conceal some sort of pattern that we should be picking up on. Aside from that, it seems that organized hostile activity within the enemy's lands has stopped."

"No life?" Etridge questioned with his pale hand. He was dressed in finely tailored gray which emphasized the elegance of his frame.

"Yes. A great deal, but all conventional. There's no power coming out of the kingdoms."

There were aerial holograms of crumbling, deserted cities, squares filled with hungry mobs cowering at the sight and sound of the aircraft, unplanted fields, canals dried up or flooding out into new swamps, the carcasses of pegasuses and leviathans bleaching like those in front of Joust Mountain except that there were no wrecked machines nearby to explain their deaths. Against this, balancing the ruin, was the life that had been suppressed by the reign of magic: trees and flowers and things that lived by themselves, rather than by the whim and fancy of men of power.

"Have you gotten anything from that eye or whatever, in the unicorn?" Etridge asked offhandedly as he organized some files on his desk, almost catching Stamp unguarded.

"I really think they tried to design too many functions into it. Internal power, transmission, analytic functions." Stamp tried to shrug off the overreaching of Special Office technology. "No wonder its signals got screwed up so quickly. Only the Office would waste their time with such gibberish."

"We had to watch it and listen to it through their eyes and ears, not our own."

Stamp shifted his weight, betraying his unease. "But it was still garbled nonsense."

"But are the signals still coming in?"

"We accidentally caught part of one three months ago. As I said, it was static and nonsense." Stamp's voice was sagging against Etridge's pressure. He had not wanted to look closely at what the transmission might have shown. It had come from inside the new silence of the enemy's world and its content had initially been determined by a fabulous beast whose existence persisted in the empty kingdoms, drawing their minds outward from the walled safety of Joust Mountain to meet it. "Why can't we just ask the Office, or whoever's running its operations now, how to listen for the eye if it's so desperately important?"

Etridge laughed behind his nobleman's hand. "That's the simplest question of all. The Office does not exist now. It's never existed. Haven't you ever asked one of its people if it did or didn't?"

Etridge's face snapped into a new alignment, slitting his eyes but failing to mask their madness. "Listen again, Stamp. I want the channels unlocked and I want the information captured and understood. I ordered that done when we discovered that it had not been shut down by the Office. I appreciate the technical difficulties involved, as well as I know how you all must regard those signals. They come from the enemy, just like all his goddamned spells and curses and bolts used to, and you're scared that you're going to get your precious hearts singed by it." Etridge read the man's thought. "Or discover that there's nothing left and it's just the call of a poor, dumb, lonely beast who hasn't been fed because we nailed its masters. I want every available scrap of information for when we go in."

"Sir?" Stamp paled noticeably under the room's fluorescent lights. "Offensive action can only be authorized by Lake Gilbert."

"Lake Gilbert has made no such authorization for one hundred years. They've forgotten how. At any rate, this will only be a reconnaissance."

Stamp had evaluated the man from Lake Gilbert correctly, for he reported nothing more than what he had been told. That alone was sufficient to freeze his superiors into a similar paralysis.

The regular services had withdrawn from the frontiers, as if they feared the silence of the enemy more than the threat of his power. Various reasons were used to justify the retreat: money was needed to rebuild the battlefields within the world (there was a circle at Thorn River where nothing had grown through the crystallized soil since the battle); policy decisions had been made to shift from active ranging to more subtle, passive methods; the battle was over, but the enemy had spitefully devastated and booby-trapped his own land so that nothing but time could make it safe again.

Aside from the budget cuts, which were real, Etridge and the other frontier commanders were delighted with this course. One spent less time looking over one's shoulder for spies from Lake Gilbert, Castle Kent or the General Accounting Office. Long-range offensive vehicles and ships were more easily requisitioned and it was simpler to keep their discoveries secret. Etridge felt that he had more room now, in back as well as in front of him.

At first, Stamp hardly noticed the hangars of Joust Mountain filling up again with hovercraft, heavy-lift helicopters and ground support ships. But some days it did seem that the worst days of the Third Perimeter and Thorn River were back.

The mood was difficult to place. He sensed none of the exhilaration that Etridge showed on progressively more frequent occasions. It was something apart from what the fortress had known before, more alive than any of its years of watching, more anxious and fearful than any of the times it had sent its garrison back to their own homes to strive against the creatures that had materialized there. Perhaps it was Etridge's madness, lying like anodized pigment over the fortress' perfect surfaces, blurring the clarity of the images that had been reflected on them for centuries.

On the upper galleries, the antennas and aerials maintained a twenty-four-hour watch, though the order for it had been re-scinded by Lake Gilbert five months before. The strain Joust Mountain was placing on the world's eastern power grids should have signaled its unauthorized activity. But then, Stamp knew, that could be ignored unless the drain was bleeding the cities white.

The evening air glowed fiercely above Joust Mountain, and there were similar fires over the opposite horizons, where White-break and Dance were. Stamp enjoyed that part of it, even if it was the old man's insanity. He felt it tugging at his heart, gradu-ally taking him from the world, away from Lake Gilbert, Castle Kent and the cities where he believed he had left so much, and turning it obsessively to the east, beyond the lands the enemy had occupied with his false religions and transparent heresies, out to where the antennas had really been looking from the very first.

Aden squatted beside the beggar. The man's limbs were covered with ulcerous sores. A cataract floated in one eye, giving the illusion of mist and hidden circuitries.

"I imagine," Aden began quietly, the journey down from the mountains having wearied him, "that the men of power have left."

"Not left, sir. They are simply gone. I perceived their going though I permitted myself to understand only part of it."

"How did they go?" Flies circled around the man's open le-sions. Out in the wasted fields, figures scraped and dug along ir-regular furrows of corn and stunted wheat.

"They fought among themselves."

"They had been doing that before."

"This time there was desperation in their acts. They sought to extract or prove"—the ancient man faltered—"some under-standing beyond the understanding shown to them during the testing of their mysteries."

"Did they find any?"

"No. None at all. What can lie beneath the truth but itself?" Like Aden, the man was very tired. "And not even they could make it otherwise. Some of them turned their powers on them-selves, others upon their retainers and familiars." The man touched himself when he said this, the expressive blind man's touch implying betrayal. "And upon their enemies. Others, upon the people." He held his withered arm out to the houses around the square and reached out to include the entire village and its surrounding field. "It was a terrible time, sir. Endless plagues, marauding creatures which had been harbored especially for the enemy were turned loose upon our lands."

"Those were probably the only places they would still work." Aden rubbed his single eye; the other was covered by a leather patch with an eye engraved on its surface.

The man nodded. "I had a form of power once myself, you know. But I kept getting it confused with what I understood, and that was not power at all but something else."

"Something more?"

"Less. It could be more than power only if you did not have it inside of yourself. You—I could not live with it that close. It was too much to be carried inside." He turned in the dust to face south. "Out there, do you see? It was the most beautiful palace where princes of one family had lived for four hundred years. Waterfalls, gardens, game forests that reached up to our walls, wise men and poets singing . . ."

"The epics of Thorn River and Heartbreak Ridge." He knew that the remark was uncalled for.

Though Aden had used his own world's names for the battles, the man seemed saddened by their mention and turned his eye downward. "I understand that those songs were sung every-where." He roused himself, as if the frailty of his body could not withstand Aden's remarks. "To your question: no, some must remain, I imagine. Fugitive, probably as mad as I." He permitted himself a laugh to show that no harm had been done. "And some of their works too."

"In the Holy City?"

"If not there, then not at all. Were you ever there?"

"You don't remember much of that, do you, Donchak?"

88

"Donchak?" shaking his head. "Ah, yes, yes. No, I do not, but I am very old, sir."

Joust Mountain's antenna arrays moved with an imaginary wind. The vague humming of their radiant energies had diminished noticeably, and the air did not smell so strongly of ozone as it usually did, though the wind was from the east.

Etridge walked before its walls with conscious dignity. A double line of hovercraft and tracked vehicles waited between him and Joust Mountain, men standing by their sides, shifting against the unaccustomed weight of side arms.

Stamp was too caught up in the sight to realize that Etridge was speaking to him: ". . . complete mapping of the areas?"

Stamp walked quickly over to him and held up a notebook. "Yes. The traces turned out to be a little more numerous than I discussed with you, but nothing which substantially alters the picture we had last week. This readout is an hour old, and the strongest concentration is still here." Stamp opened the notebook, selected a small-scale map and pointed to where a great number of shaded radii intersected. "Area Twelve, the Holy City."

"Holy, I'm sure, only in comparison to the rest of the other kingdoms." Etridge was amused. Behind him, a loose formation of wind ships rode the thermals over the dead lake, engines out, spiraling lazily up into the morning.

Aden watched the imagist for an hour before he slipped him a coin. "A beauty," he said. In response the man shut his eyes and then plucked up the thought that Aden held at the edge of his mind.

He moved his hands, and the air between them shimmered and condensed into the shape of a woman. She was very well shaped, and this was clear despite the loose robes she had been dressed in. A good imagist knew the touches that compliment memory, and those which blatantly exaggerate it and thereby offend. She was tall, which was also correct, and with fine delicate features overlain by pale skin that was nearly translucent. The nose was small, and the eyes hovered between green and slate and blue.

Aden nodded approvingly. The man was very good, much better than the sort the smaller towns usually got by with. But the most common subject of a public imagist was lost loves. They acquired, if only from sheer repetition, some facility in gathering from a man's mind what he chose to remember, rather than any great truth about what the person might have really been like.

When magic was whole, the best imagists were prized by even the mightiest men of power. They could read secrets of startling depth or shape extravagant fantasies from the surfaces of other men's thought and then build them into visions of unbearable intensity. Not surprisingly, most of them succumbed to their own talent, drugging themselves as their visions fed and multiplied on each other.

Aden waved the image away. As he expected, the sight of her touched him, but not deeply. The magic of the imagist functioned like the gunsight's marvelous technology. Both allowed him to see Gedwyn, but only from a distance that existed in addition to those of time and memory. Both reduced and quantified her, both could be dismissed with a gesture.

He felt something like relief when the picture was gone. It was as if her memory, which might otherwise grow out of control, had been removed from his heart. It would grow back again, but each time it would be proportionately weaker.

He was growing, acquiring a manly depth of memories and history, but did not know why there should be a feeling of self-disgust left in the place the imagist had taken the picture of Gedwyn from.

Aden threw the man two more coins and smiled stiffly. The men around them made comic groans that he had not permitted a more explicit insight into his affections.

"Allow us the design of mystery and power." In ordinary times this would have been a joke, for common people could not bear to see such things any more than a street imagist would be able to conjure them.

"You are from the past, my sir," the imagist replied in a professionally respectful voice, scooping up the money. "There are none left."

"I have been away from my home, and did not know that the question is no longer asked."

"Only rarely." Pain crossed the faces of the imagist and his other patrons; some of them rubbed their jaws in their hands and drifted back into the street. Still, the man seemed to feel an obligation to his trade and for monies already received. He became silent again, moving his hands until the outlines of an onion-domed temple formed, stained from the weather, alabaster windows blank and dark. It faded quickly and was replaced by another picture, this one of a slim aircraft, propeller-driven and like the one that had flown over Aden in the mountains. The plane wove and turned like a weaver's shuttle between the man's hands.

Aden attempted to look shocked for it had been heresy to so portray the devices of the enemy. "Apologies, my sir. It was all I could show you." The plane evaporated. Aden saw that only he and the imagist were left in the tiny park. The others had left when the temple had appeared and then started to vanish. "I took it more from my own mind than yours."

The man was staring directly into Aden's good eye. As he did so, his face relaxed into a familiar weariness. Aden said: "Office?" slurring the word so that he hardly recognized it.

"My sir?" with forced astonishment. He whirled his hands again, and the picture of an eye formed between them, suspended in a web of copper wires. It lasted a second before going. "Your money's worth, my sir?"

The imagist's village was bitterly cold in winter, and the fields and ruined palaces near it were encrusted with ice. But when the wind died and the sun was not hidden by storm clouds, people still found it pleasant to come out into the wide, barren streets to spy on their neighbor's food supply and conduct themselves as they had before, when great enchantments protected them from the weather.

The imagist was out at his usual place, the hood of his sheep-skin cloak thrown back for the sun, practicing the same tired round of illusions for the same crowd of idlers and bored farmers. He took care to make a picture different each time the same person requested it, and many in the village remembered his pictures better than the actual events on which they had originally been based.

He sometimes thought of himself as not only the shaper of the village's memories but as one who created its present as well. He knew this to be a fantasy and the progressive intensity with which it asserted itself troubled him. He had thought of going home, but that would not have solved the problem of illusion. If anything, it would have only intensified it, because that world, unlike the one he presently inhabited, had not been stripped of all its closest dreams. It still abounded, he guessed, in thought and life enough to bloat his imagination. He decided that he was safer in this world, where almost everything of the heart and mind had been carried off by the magicians when they fled.

On this morning, however, he was thinking of his own world, testing his memory with the picture of severely uniformed men who never smiled and from whom light never shone. His audience had no idea what he was doing and thought it only to be some long, diverting myth about the imaginary time before their War.

Because of his absorption, the imagist was not particularly surprised when the gray man edged his way forward through the crowd and threw him an unfamiliar coin. It merely seemed that one of his pictures had found a mirror in the people around him.

The man was of medium height and the skin lay easily about his mild features: blue eyes, long, artistic hands and fingers unscarred and uncalloused, well-fitting clothes with archaic lapel flashes on the jacket. He smelled oppressively clean.

"You wish to see, my sir?"

The other man inclined his head. "The design of power." He had at least studied some of the local idiom. The imagist decided the man was real, or at least an illusion sustained by someone else.

The picture was an easy one for the young man carried its

component parts constantly before him, as if he were afraid they might slip from his grasp if they were not held so tightly.

He began with a line, formed it into a triangle, which thereupon expanded into a square, to a pentagon, hexagon, octagon, a sphere growing tangents that curved off into diminishing radius arcs that, before the image was completed, hinted at Llwyellan Functions.

"I had wished the image to be yours rather than mine."

"I have no images of that sort left to me, nor do the people around you. Yours was the only one I could find." The man looked up the street and the imagist caught the picture of armed men also dressed in gray, reflected on the surfaces of his mind. Beyond them were vehicles painted white and olive, caked with frozen mud and dust and much too large to fit into the village's streets. The imagist noted that all of them carried one or more antennas, mostly dished units or flattened cylinders, and found the one that was examining him.

He felt his hands wavering in their movements, and stopped before the image disappeared into abstraction by itself.

"Anything else, old man?" Another person dressed like the first, but taller and with fiercely ascetic features had come up to him.

The imagist sensed his own fear as strongly as when the men of power had begun to leave or destroy themselves. He instinctively closed his eyes and searched the land around the the village. He found other things in the silence but he was now badly shaken and could not identify them. "Yes."

"A picture then," the second man ordered too loudly. "A picture of the powers in this land!" The younger man looked embarrassed.

"Lost the knack so soon? Allow me to assist." A third man joined them and handed the speaker a green notebook. The imagist heard the sound of motors grinding at the still air. A low fog of crystallized ice rose from under the plenum skirt of the hovercraft parked at the end of the street, lending it the appearance of slow burning. The man raised his hand and pointed to the northeast. "You may find some form of power . . ."

"Sir!" the imagist shouted as the picture blasted across his mind.

The bolt hit and leveled the block of houses on the opposite side of the park. There was no sound or shock wave, just an intense heat that drove them back behind the nearest wall.

"No power? Goddamn bastard!" The second man grabbed the imagist by the front of his cloak and nearly lifted him off his feet.

His mouth working through the usual signs of terror, the other man yelled, "I don't understand this. It can't be this! It hasn't for years!"

Etridge smiled back and dropped the other man. "Relieved, Stamp?" he hissed as another block of houses and godowns detonated. Then he stepped back and began trotting along the undamaged side of the street, back to the vehicles. Stamp followed uncertainly.

The imagist and the man who had brought the book to Etridge stayed for a moment. They saw that the fires left by the two bolts were made from extraordinary colors; despite the rush of heat released by their impact, they now danced above the ruins without warmth, as if they had used themselves up all at once and remained only as an after-image in their eyes. One or two people staggered from the houses, seemingly unaware of the gold and scarlet flames that were eating at the backs of their skulls.

The third bolt consumed the burning people, the imagist and the man beside him.

Stamp looked back in time to see this. More bolts hit the village and their fires spiraled upward and joined together. "Firestorm!" he yelled to Etridge as they ran through the village gate.

"Not melodramatic enough. Not enough drama. No fuel for their dreams," Etridge shouted back. The engines of the hovercraft and tanks accelerated in front of them. Light half-tracks scattered at right angles to the road, side-looking radars moving in nervous jerks to stay fixed on the burning village.

They reached the lead hovercraft. It lifted off as they boarded, dipping slightly as its gyroscopes came into phase. Three identical units floated backward, away from the village.

The individual fires kept twisting together until the density of their light cast a shadow against the sun. Branches grew downward from points a hundred meters from the ground, and as they watched, the pillar assumed shape and animation.

"Splendid!" Etridge remarked to the bridge crew when he saw this. "Nearly the same thing they tried at Foxblind. If it really is, it'll have the shape of some wonderful beast, like a minotaur or such. They're incapable of thinking in terms of simple power, always anthropomorphizing this or that so each act has the personal mark of the man behind it. What do you say, Stamp? Two to one it's a minotaur."

"The same device was employed at Thorn River . . ."—trying to appear knowledgeable.

Etridge's face went through a sequence of closed and guarded expressions. "Yes. Except there, they used hundreds of those fire things, and each one had the shape and the face of the last person it killed. We didn't know how to fight them then."

Dust swirled outside the hovercraft's windows as it slid backward. The fiery column danced in the half-light, seeming to grow in rough proportion to the distance they traveled away from it. The planes of Etridge's face matched the lines of the craft's bridge and the flanking turrets on either side of it. "Pointless melodrama. Wasted effort!"

Two men behind him received the input from the circling tanks and from the antennas on the four main ships.

"They never seem to learn or understand," Etridge muttered over the engines. "They always give us enough time."

"Sir, the second unit thinks they have something. They want to experiment."

Etridge nodded, the man spoke into a microphone, and the hovership to their right tentatively opened fire.

All four ships stopped their rearward movement and watched as it continued shooting. Two kilometers away, the fire-beast detached itself from the village and began striding toward them. Etridge's smile came back when the bull's head defined itself.

"Not working very well," Etridge commented absently. "Anyone else read the input differently?" Responding light, chromium against the fire-minotaur's yellow and red, angled out from antennas on the two hoverships on their left. Similar lines were drawn from three tanks racing around the northern side of the creature.

An officer came up behind them. "Rather different from previous stuff. But we're running interference patterns with the scatter antennas too, and I think that might do it."

"All right. Let's get closer."

Stamp placed both his hands on the grab rail and moved his feet apart. He had read and studied the phenomena the men of power had conjured for centuries, but his actual dealings with them had been as remote as most of his contemporaries, those who had grown into the war's world after Thorn River. He had always seen the wizards' might and their own through the reductive prisms of computers.

Now that they were moving forward, diminishing perspective and the beast's own increasing powers made it grow alarmingly in the windscreen's aldiss rings. The glass darkened automatically to compensate for the brilliance.

"Additional presences behind the subject," a man at the console called out.

"Close on them." Etridge's smile widened, breaking his facial planes into patterns of broken glass.

The driver accelerated the ship. Stamp saw more lines of the chrome light emerge from the top of the windscreen and join with the fire from the other craft at a point on the creature's neck. Blocking radiations combined with its own indefinite structure and made it difficult to tell if the beast's raging gestures expressed any problematic agony or were merely part of its slow, dancing attack.

If there was only some sound, Stamp thought, not just the eternally competent murmuring of our own engines and the afternoon light from the armored windows.

Etridge is enjoying this, he also thought, far more than the ship itself was; to it, and to most of its crew, the menace and wonder of the beast was that of an enemy, no more unique or terrible than a rifle squad or a fighter-bomber. Among some old combat units there had been a saying to the effect that "there is only one kind of dead."

They were all older than himself, and had fought this enemy for years before Thorn River. They were absorbed in the ship's dials and scopes; the driver and fire control personnel looked at the minotaur through target and range grids projected onto the windows in front of them. Only he and Etridge had no assigned station and there was nothing in front of them to block or polarize the fire-creature's power. Stamp wondered if the two of them were succumbing to it.

"Cavalry behind it," the man called out again.

"Nothing more?"

"No sir." The man paused to examine the readout. "And these're much simpler. Tanks on the right report they've already eliminated one or two."

"Good. The survivors may be throwing their palace guards against us, Stamp."

Stamp mumbled something he hoped would not show his concern. Two silver dots appeared far above the minotaur. Simultaneously wiith their sighting, a nimbus of visual anomalies edged the beast's outline.

Every vehicle in the column, except the lightest half-tracks, joined in spinning the cool, sharp lines that wavered and bent only where they passed through the giant.

The hovercraft on their right paused and then resumed gunfire. This time its ammunition was perfectly suited to destruction in the dimension which the creature's life and energy came from. The shells began cratering its body, disrupting the sustaining life that the enemy poured into it, freezing its fire so that it could splinter apart like dense red crystal.

The other main units joined in, replacing their inquisitory lights with gunfire. Stamp felt a release as the reports thudded against the cabin walls and the creature finally bellowed out its pain.

Etridge anticipated his question: "That's not the minotaur, Stamp, but the despair of the man who built it"—turning smoothly to the younger men and then back to the village.

"We've shown him something which he'd rather not have seen. Haven't we, Anderton?" The fire control officer accepted the compliment without any sign, keeping his eyes on his ranging scopes. "And now our survivor of power finds that he can't let his little vision go. We've contained his puppet and we've also snared his sustaining powers. Listen to him!"

Etridge crossed over to the right side of the cabin and slid open a window. The cabin was filled with the deafening sound of the batteries and over them, the long pathetic wailing of the fire-minotaur as the chromium lines shackled it, dragging it to its knees and holding it still for their barrage.

The bridge crew clamped their earphones more tightly to their heads and tried to ignore it. Stamp could not, but found it less unnerving than the linear hum of the ship's engines.

The creature lost its form and dissolved back into the low, brilliant fires it had arisen from twelve minutes ago. "Short glory," Etridge said. There was a line of armored deaths, carrying lances made of darkness and mounted on gryphons, behind the flattened village. "Ah! The costume ball!" and clapped his hands together.

The driver edged the throttles forward with what seemed to Stamp to be needless theatricality.

The line stretched for at least two kilometers. They stood utterly, stupidly motionless as the light and the surgical gunfire concentrated on the rider at each end. They refused to move as they were enveloped in Joust Mountain's merciless understanding, refused to show emotion or come to the aid of their fellows when their limbs turned to powder and the gateways their lances defined between their own world and that of their master were brutally slammed snut.

"Are they alive?" Stamp breathed.

"Alive enough for us to murder them. Like I said, Stamp, that is their failing. They must always personify their powers and try to make them the reflection of their own thoughts."

"They're artists. They have to do it that way. It's the only way they understand . . ."

98

"They understand nothing! That's what they think is the base of their power. Ignorance made into a religion."

The four ships advanced into the village. It had been consumed to feed the creature's minutes of birth and life, but the ships elevated to three meters to be safe. The remaining fires played against their sides, impotent and sucked dry by the ship's light.

"Now . . ." As Etridge spoke to the driver, the hovercraft on their right collided with a thick column of masonry; it had been wrapped in a fire which Anderton's instruments quickly analyzed and found to be of the same composition as the minotaur. Too late; no one had been looking at the fires around them.

The burning rock cut into the ship's left side, shearing away the plenum skirt and gouging into its understructure. The window on that side of Etridge's ship was still open; the screech of tearing metal and ceramic armor hit them along with a last, undefined echo of the minotaur.

The wounded hovercraft spun to the right and dug its nose into the burning ruins. The other ships, although they had identified the fire, did not shoot for fear of hitting it. Its metal structure ignited in five of the non-visual dimensions, turning white and slagging into a glittering lake.

The fire penetrated the engines and fuel cells. The glass on the right side of Etridge's ship went black except for the open vent window; the light from it drilled into Stamp's retina, threatening to dissolve his heart.

"God, kill it!" Etridge screamed to the computers. The three remaining craft swung their antennas and weapons downward along their own flanks. The batteries went automatic, driving shells of unimaginably complex structures into the remaining humps and masses which hinted at animate power. Gyroscopes rocked violently against the ships' roll axes to compensate for the hammering recoil and concussions rising up alongside the hulls.

Stamp dove at the window and slammed it shut against the physical pressure of the exterior light.

The hovercraft bathed each other in radiations and shells they themselves only half understood. That was enough.

99

The glass cleared. The fires were gone, flattened into common reality. Only the line of cavalry stood before them; the vanished ship was forgotten. All three hoverships leveled their batteries upon the northern end of the line, accidentally crushing the nearest tank, and swept along it.

The noise was similar to that of the minotaur and its dying, but now the windows and ventilators were closed and it had the distance of memory. "His most truly beloved," Etridge observed with forced calm. As the distance closed, they could recognize skull faces and shreds of putrefied flesh hanging from seams in their cuirasses and greaves. "The minotaur was a robot. Our man of power gave nothing to it which was of his own but some life. But look how he must love those things. Look, Stamp! Can you see starlight shining through, no, inside their lances! He's given them power of their own. He must trust them greatly."

"We've hit the fourth unit," the driver shouted over the muffled howling. He pointed to his left and the rest of the crew reflexively followed his hand. The hovercraft farthest from them was drawing away, near side tilted down, escaping air driving it across their path against the rudders in full opposite lock. "She'll ground!"

Speed brakes snapped open on their ship and the one next to them. They dug into the air and slowed them enough for the damaged ship to arc in front of them. Its guns and antennas were all pointed at the line of deaths, at maximum elevation raking them and shattering individuals as if they had been made from ivory glass.

"Look at this." Etridge's voice was flat and unemotional in comparison to when he had spoken of the enemy. Then, he had sounded as if he were about to take a rival's love; but the dying craft presented him with no mystery or challenge. The reasons and causes for its actions had been understood before the Wizards' War began. The ship could have never served as the gateway Etridge sought.

He watched the terror spread before the careening ship. Its windows were solid black, so he could not gauge its crew's reaction.

Its magazines detonated and a long club of fire and hard radiation descended on the southern third of the line. It drowned them, burning them from the inside, cremating their interior blankness and turning their peculiar nights into ash.

The cabin darkened again to protect the men from the other ship's arsenal. Ventilator guards snapped shut and nickel steel shields locked over them. The silence returned, now absolute, and the only light was from red battle lanterns.

Navigation and fire control grids were projected across the closed windows to guide them. The completeness of the schematic diagrams showed how thoroughly these enemies were understood. Energy graphs, spectral analysis, frequency and dimensional readings sped crisply along the borders of the windows.

The computers anticipated Etridge's anger. The other ship appeared as a schematic on the left side windows; dense columns of information showed that it was destroying the northern end of the line. Etridge's ship concentrated on the middle, and at a range of one hundred meters it broke.

The coherency of the line fragmented. Individual deaths fell apart or burst into saffron flame or ran straight into the guns of the two ships and the flanking vehicles. Others ran to the east. The instruments traced the lines of power that drew them and, one by one, cut them.

They passed the spot where the second ship had touched down. Readings indicated a shallow gouge in the earth, at right angles to their line of travel, and fatally high radiation levels, but little else.

The windows cleared. Eighty-three deaths remained before the hovercraft, most of them charred and shredded. Their mounts were similarly mauled, some running comically on two opposed legs, the stumps of their other legs repeating the movements of running, their balance presumably held by the same power that sustained the lives of their riders.

Stamp could see stars inside their lances, more absence than presence, as they swayed drunkenly against the gun and light-fire. He felt himself sickening, equally from the grotesquery of the spectacle and from an overwhelming sense of pity and sorrow. "They're done," he whispered, and was astonished when Etridge raised his hand and ordered cease fire.

Instead of turning about and attending to their wounded, Etridge added: "Pace them. This distance is fine."

"They're dead."

"Quite. I'd say they were before we attacked. Now they are truly dead. That might be death they hold in their hands." Etridge smiled. "Mr. Anderton, please direct our antennas and those of the other unit entirely to those fellows. I don't think our man of power has anything else for us today. And see if you can get those two wind ships down low enough for some close looking."

The officer behind them spoke into his microphone.

"They've been understood, sir. We know them!" Stamp was aware of how tenuous his ground might be. "The graphs have all placed and fixed them on the spectrums. Why not wipe them out and end it? The others . . ."

"The others should be watching them as closely as we are. As you should be, Stamp." Etridge was parental; he might actually enjoy Stamp's little treason. "We know them and the chemical and atomic reactions that sustain them. See?" He pointed to patterns of luminous dials along the right side of the cabin. "We know how they're dying. We have wounded them sufficiently to give their own form of death enough momentum to proceed on its own. They are heading for that death, real and absolute. But we musn't hurry them. No, no need for that. Just pat them along with a little flash of light or a kiss of the Mountain's choicest amatol, just enough to keep the bastards moving along that path so we can watch them running, watch how their gifts of power run off and try to hide themselves."

At irregular intervals one of the antennas above them or on the other ship went active. Quanta of light drove into the functioning riders who were not dying at an appropriate speed.

They followed them until the smoke from the village and the wreck of the first hovercraft was below the horizon. They fell individually, taking with them whatever plan they might have had to attack the ships and the tank column. Etridge directed the ships to pass over them as they dropped. Articulated arms inside the plenum chambers snatched samples of bone and armor and chitinous skin as they died and transmuted back into the elements and energies from which they had been formed.

The ventilators opened. The screaming of the last deaths entered the cabin, instantly captured on wall-mounted oscilloscopes and written into spinning globes of frozen helium. Later, the computers at Joust Mountain would take this information, their agonies and pain, and relate them to all the mysteries they had accumulated over three hundred years of watching, understanding their meanings as they had been reflected in the carbonization of battlefield flowers and in the blinding faces of distant stars. Their inquiries had to be made on such a scale for the ways of men of power were vast and infinitely devious.

"Bring the planes down and block them," Etridge said.

They maintained the distance, devouring the stragglers as they fell. Stamp saw the aircraft turning into the wind far ahead of them.

After ten minutes of casual pursuit, he could see the two aircraft on the ground. They faced the approaching ships, noses high and resting on their tail wheels, momentarily suggesting foreshortened crucifixes. The featureless plain gave no hint as to their size; Stamp knew the wingspread of each one was over ninety meters. The wings themselves were antennas. Everything that Etridge had chosen to accompany him was devoted to perception.

They played their questioning radiations back and forth against the hoverships, through the knot of ghostly cavalry. Opportunities for such examinations occurred only when magic erupted within the heartlands of its enemy's world, and there had not been such a thing since Foxblind. The tape banks and helium spheres choked on the rush of information that poured into them.

Etridge was pleased. When there was less than seventy meters between them and the aircraft, he said to Anderton, "End them all."

Light, this time in pale, fan-shaped arrays, beat against twenty-two survivors. The planes laid down their own light too, and the deaths faltered and dove into the ground. Some of them melted into the surface ice, hazings of steam rising from under their disintegrating bodies.

The two hovercraft deployed their drag skids and eased to the ground. Etridge waited a moment and stepped outside. Stamp followed and was overwhelmed by the smell. He had not imagined that anything could have so fouled winter air.

The wind ship crews jumped down from the wings and strolled into the wreckage. Every one of them carried hand analyzers of one sort or another, machines that tested the discoveries of the other machines. They chipped at the fairyland armor with geologist's picks, placed samples in glass bottles and watched as the fragments cracked and vaporized the glass. These fragments, in turn, were deposited in successive containers until something was found to hold them.

There was some joking, but most of the conversation was taken up with numbers and code references. Except for Etridge: "Is that death?" He pointed with his boot at one of the black lances the riders carried; its owner was dust and damp rot beside it.

"Will it kill you? Probably. Its form and composition derive from . . ." Anderton's voice, flat and metallic over the hovercraft's loudspeaker.

"No! Is it death? True and actual death. Not just a device that could cause it." Etridge stared down at the tapering shaft; it appeared more of a hole or tear in the ground than something that lay on top of it.

Stamp squatted and found the perspectives the thing reported to his eyes violently contradictory. Starlike objects flickered inside of it, but these were fading.

"No, sir," Anderton answered after a pause. Stamp imagined that he sounded as disappointed as Etridge looked; but that was probably the effect of the scene and the amplifier.

"The lines are gone," Anderton continued. "Our man of power has left."

"Before we told him too much about himself." Etridge addressed the hovercraft.

"That may have happened. The sounds of those things couldn't have been entirely their own. As you said about the minotaur."

Etridge stopped listening and turned to Stamp. "If that has happened, if he has left us now, how can we follow him? How will we know where to look?"

He's really asking me, thought Stamp, and held his ignorance like a precious secret.

Aden recognized more landmarks as he left the ruins of Clairendon and neared the Holy City. The fields, as with the rest of the enemy's lands, were blasted and sterile, waiting for the rains and the ancient, alien seeds they would bring. The ruins of fabulous palaces and villas sat against charred hillsides or along the drained channels of rivers that the magicians had summoned only for their sound. He remembered how, when he fled the City, the towers of these great houses had risen above the forests, flaunting their gardens and erotic sculptures against the patient watching of Joust Mountain and Dance.

A few of the shells hinted at inhabitation, if not by princes, then possibly by powers which had detached themselves from their makers to become self-sustaining, as the gravitational fields of celestial black holes had been thought to be.

Shadowed lights could be glimpsed behind the stained glass remnants of windows. There were also signal fires on isolated hill forts, and Aden occasionally thought he could see the sky flickering and glowing as it had over the Holy City. But this was not much; these mysteries were not being swallowed up by his world's understanding but by the emptiness around them.

He now walked through a field becoming lush with spring grass and the wildflowers of his world. There was a small herd of pegasuses grazing there, strong and powerful. Their caparisons were slitted to allow free movement to their wings; these rested against their flanks, colored like golden cock pheasants. Their armor was meant for flight, being limited to quilting under the caparisons and a crinet of silver mesh.

All their saddles were empty. Aden guessed they had been the scouts of a man of power, such squadrons usually affecting the most extravagant liveries, as he guessed that all their uniforms and bravado and the power they had served had been explained and unraveled by Joust Mountain. Because their task had been reconnaissance, as his had been, they would have discovered their own reality and that of their master before anyone else.

Anderton pointed to a diamond fixed on the moving map grids and reference lines. "I thought we were going to be the only ones out here." He went on with ponderous, Border-bred irony. "And there, and there, and there again."

"But nothing like this," said Etridge, moving closer and pointing to the first diamond.

"No, sir," referring to the rows of dials and linear readouts to his right. "It almost seems to be one of ours. Except . . ."

"Well?"

"Multiple fixtures and nets within the subject's cranial structure. The readings are indefinite, but we can't hope for much more at these distances."

"Active?"

"No, not for some time. Conductance indicates that the nets haven't been used for anything for over two years. It's all very well hidden," Anderton concluded, hoping for approval.

"The Special Office used to wire up people like that." Etridge seemed to be addressing the rows of dials.

"The Office has closed."

"It never existed. Right, Anderton?"

The other man looked to Stamp for assistance; Stamp turned away. "That's supposed to have been the way of outfits like that."

"Like what?"

Anderton fidgeted with his headpiece. "The undercover people, the spies . . ."

"Imagists," Stamp mumbled involuntarily.

"Ah, my aide was watching after all." He returned to Anderton, whose look of relief accordingly vanished. "As you say, that is the way of outfits like that. That one is closed, but that act of organizational death is, itself, an admission of the life they steadfastly denied. Interesting, don't you think?"

Stamp saw Anderton mustering his courage in the set of his facial muscles. "That can't matter much to us. If the thing existed, all its lying couldn't change that fact."

"Our opinion is secondary to what *they* were thinking of themselves," Stamp cut in, irritated with the way Etridge was playing with the man. The strategy of his world permitted no fascination with paradox and contradiction for its own sake, and Anderton was innocent of such things. "People listen mostly to themselves."

"And eventually one comes to speak and think in a warped shorthand, comprehensible only to one's self or to others who live in the same dream," Etridge finished for him. He smiled his approval to Stamp and this increased the other's anger. "That's what our princes of power did until we accidentally showed them a more captivating dream, the one we're sleeping through right now."

"Sir?" Anderton was honestly puzzled at the equation of his own world with that of the enemy.

"Don't worry. Our dream's the right one. Isn't it, Stamp?"

"It appears to be the only one, sir." Stamp turned on his heel and left the bridge, Etridge looking after him as if it had been some kind of triumph.

"Get on the channels to Lake Gilbert and ask them if there're files open on the person with the readings you've picked up at that first position."

Anderton nodded to a man farther down on the console. Circles of yellow and green light switched on and then off, and the other man pressed his earphones to his head. "The files are closed," he reported after some minutes. Anderton busied himself with his instruments before he could be drawn back into his commander's disturbing way of discussing a target with wires in its head. Range, speed, weight, respiration, molecular composition: the man obviously existed, so what was the use of talk of non-existence?

Aden knew that the wires and grids that remained implanted in his body were without power sources. They had no way to gather information from around him, nor did they have any place to store signals from the Office, had it, too, been functioning.

Because of this, Aden first suspected that one of the pegasus riders had survived. There was nothing visual, but rather tentative movements and half-formed ideas turning like shadows beneath his conscious mind. He vaguely connected this feeling with those the unicorn and its attendant had inspired in him years ago. But the grazing pegasuses had no intimidating cathedral to help propel his mood from discomfort to terror.

Also, there seemed to be only one concept now, quite different from the spectrum-wide wave fronts of thought that the unicorn had hinted at. It swam out of reach, its texture metallic and sharp for all its lack of definition.

Aden touched his fingers to the sides of his hand. The old patchwork of wires branched out from the inside of his skull through an occipital hole grommeted with a ring of pure gold. His thick, ash-colored hair made the pattern invisible to one who did not already know of its presence.

The wires moved under his fingers. Again, so small and elusive that he might fairly judge it as imagination.

"That's over, gone," he muttered to the pegasuses. Two of them looked at him in momentary agreement.

The sound of his own voice startled him, as if it had suddenly revealed him to covert watchers. But he had been in the open since he had left Dance. Hiding was impossible, particularly when he had entered the abandoned kingdoms of magic. If he had not been seen, it was because no one was looking for him.

Now there was something. The Office, perhaps, attempting to contact him in its appropriately non-existent way, to call him back or to urge him on.

Or the pegasus riders, centering him in cross hairs drawn with fire in the open air, preparing spells and enchantments of terrible finality.

Or his world had come already, and he had only felt the brush of its inquisitory antennas as they reviewed the power and meaning of everything left alive in the enemy's land.

The last of the three was the most logical. It was proper that his world should come and occupy the vacuum left by the defeat of magic, thus preserving symmetry and balance. But he knew the occupation would be total when it came and that it would find no reason to stop with what might soon be understood as a minor victory.

Individual wires pulsed. His conception of his world's victory shrank as he began to suspect the dimensions of the field on which it had been fought.

The pegasuses' gorgeous ornamentation became the rags of refugees too inconsequential for the forces of either side to destroy. When he was a child, he had watched creatures like them struggling along the roads leading from Thorn River. They had been burned and starved and brutalized by forces so alien that their bodies seemed unsure as to what sort of death was called for. The pegasuses, grazing in their rich field, were the same, for their eyes had been turned to cinders by the things they had witnessed. They had been deserted by their commanders and their creation, and there was nothing left for them. But they, unlike the victims of Thorn River, or of the Third Perimeter or Foxblind, were not yet fully aware of this, so they persisted in their wonder and existence.

Aden touched the long-barreled automatic in its holster. The Office had fashioned it so that it could change the nature and composition of its ammunition in the magazine. The Office, however, had purposely made it fragile and needlessly complex. It was machined to tolerances more suited to match competition than field service. He was not even sure he could remember how to work it.

He resumed walking. The wires continued to pulse for some moments and then left him alone but for the thought of the Office, orbiting through its own strange, self-created nighttime, pondering its own existence and never wishing to approach any answer.

Aden smiled tensely. His skin stretched against the eye patch, hiding its edges and making the stylized eye engraved on it appear to be his own: brown cornea, black iris, brown pupil.

The riverbed was carpeted with sword grass. Scarlet and yellow wildflowers spotted the greenness. Small trees that survived the spring runoff thumped against the plenum skirts of the two hovercraft. Like Joust Mountain, they were flawlessly white, arrogantly perfect despite the dirt and fires that the kingdoms had hurled at them.

The column had waited after the first village, conversing with the computers of their home until they understood what had happened to them. Then they buried what the powers had left of their dead.

Etridge kept asking about the Special Office. Nothing obtrusive, just occasional inquiries as to what this closed Office file or that sealed Office report might have had to say about the way the enemy had moved or what its dark lances might have actually been composed of.

As they had supposed, the animating forces behind the fire-minotaur and the dead cavalries were basically the same as those used for ages, with only minor variations drawn from one or two neglected corners of the parallel spectrums. How they had managed to come upon the column undetected required more study.

When the study group at Saart finally understood it and fabricated machineries to duplicate it, Lake Gilbert broadcast this knowledge to places where the remaining men of power might be listening from. Seven thousand kilometers from the Holy City the castle of the prince who had carried out the attack and committed his last and most favorite retainers to its success, turned from the sunlight of which his father had built it, to stone and then to rust, and then to slag.

A trio of wind ships hovered above the castle, observing its disintegration. The acuity of their watching nearly took the mystery of the castle's death away from its dying prince and exiled both him and it in the world they could not conceive of fully enough to hate.

Etridge was pleased with the course of the mission. Stamp made an opposing show of his displeasure, hoping to find the point at which Etridge would drop his insane dialogues and simply accuse him of insubordination or treason.

The kingdoms, however, continually provided them diverting nests of lingering magic. Stamp celebrated each irregular assault that hit them. Etridge was similarly prideful when they slowed and then understood each one.

"Reductio ad imperium" had been scrawled around the base of one of the ship's antenna mounts. Each man saw the other staring at it in odd moments, and saw him regarding it as his own. Gradually Stamp came to attach a tremendous weight of bitterness and irony to it. Etridge found it a perfect expression of the soldier's ethos in this war, just triumphant enough to distract that soldier from how far the phrase begged to be taken.

Etridge leaned close to the windscreen, enjoying the torrent of grass passing under the ship. A ranging mast extended twenty meters outward from the leading edge of the ship like a bowsprit, anticipating drops and irregularities in the ground's contours. The smooth, relentless movement put him in mind of his own obsessions. He considered how the appeal of the mysteries and their solving, one by one, acquired their own propulsive force, gradually forming the conviction that the horizon might not prove to be an eternally receding one.

Why, he marveled to his own reflection, did Stamp seem so repelled by such a suggestion? Certainly the searching was the greatest part, not the thought they might someday actually arrive at a complete and literal understanding of the universe. But, he also permitted himself, if such a position could be reached, it might include an understanding of primary creative forces, gods, if you will, and in so understanding them, encompass them and take their measure.

He could not hope to do things like that. He was a soldier, not a theologian or a philosopher. On cue, the jumble of misconnected nerve endings in his right side that the observation of Thorn River had cost him, burned lightly. Not badly, but enough to remind him of that place's terror, and that this business of understanding and unraveling had to continue. If men did not continue it, if they allowed the momentum of their victorious strategy to dissipate, then they would have shown themselves to be as careless and blind as the god that created them.

How: that was what they were discovering, but very seldom the *why*. Transmutation, parthenogenesis, animation of the dead, generation of love, psychokinesis, all the dread mechanisms the enemy had used from Heartbreak Ridge to Thorn River. With each understanding, they revealed themselves to be only the operant expressions of deeper and more complex motivations. He recalled an Office memorandum on the subject which he had read years ago, but could not attach any great importance to what it had said.

The only thing one could do, Etridge considered, was to attempt to understand everything. The sum of these understandings might eventually equal and then exceed the understanding of the single motive for all of it.

Etridge laughed as he visualized the personifications of eschatology and existentialism (both comic, lumbering giants, the former dressed in priest's robes and the latter naked) running on convergent arcs, colliding and merging into a single creature whose chief distinction was in the possession of two backsides: the Meaning of the Universe. He forced down his chuckling when he saw that the bridge crew was staring at him.

The valley where he had seen the pegasuses widened out into rolling plains of wild wheat and prairie grass. Groves of cottonwood trees marked the turning points of drainages and streams.

The sky above him was immense. It swallowed the clouds and all other presences within and below it, and turned down the edges of the horizon until one felt one's self trying to balance on one foot to avoid falling and rolling down to it forever. It was nothing like he remembered it to have been. Perhaps the men of power, jealous of the sky's presumption, had kept it shrunken and contained. They had exiled the ocean from Cape St. Vincent because it displeased them. Surely the sky could not have posed significantly greater problems. He wondered how it might have been done, and his face tightened when he thought that if it had been accomplished, then there were machines at Lake Gilbert and Castle Kent working at the problem, translating the gestures and alchemies and ancient disciplines into the precise language of the parallel spectrums, which any man could learn to speak in its single dialect.

On the opposite bank of a stream he saw the imprints of tracked vehicles, a meter across. The tracks led in from the west, followed the stream for a short while and then turned to the south, along his intended path.

Diesel fuel and grease stained the grass. For a moment he found its smell pleasant. At least the vacuum left by the men of power was being filled by something.

One of the tracks passed over a crushed dragon's egg in the semicircle of its stone nest. The unhatched embryo had struggled halfway out of the cracked egg. The ants had carried off its eyes and tongue, leaving the chitinous outer skin; the sun had shriveled its filmy wings and turned the emerging diamonds on its breast and tail to dull pebbles. Once, Aden knew, dragons had been as immortal and as invulnerable as any magician.

He found the first tank the next day. It was hardly recognizable as such, being a mass of crystallized metal shards and melted slag. The wreckage suggested rapid alternations of freezing and burning, shifting back and forth across the spectral planes too quickly for the vehicle's defenses to lock onto any single manifestation of the enemy's assault.

The ground near the wreck was chewed up and littered with shapes Aden assumed to be bones and weapons. He picked up one such fragment and found a dryad's head carved upon it. Her eyes seemed to move even when he held it perfectly still; the face studied him in this way for a minute and then closed its eyes.

Aden put the fragment in his pocket and looked around. Far away, again to the south, dust and smoke rose below a spindle-shaped chunk of rock, floating above the prairie. There was a castle built atop it, and the distance could not diminish its delicacy or its outrageous fantasy. White marble minarets braced against the wind by buttresses of malachite and onyx marked the borders of the island and rose about the central keep. That, too, was of white stone, underlain with the captured light of the moon so that, although there was darkness underneath the island, the castle itself held no shadows.

Following the tracks, Aden saw a line of eight large vehicles and several smaller ones strung out along a ridge a kilometer from the air-island. Three of the tanks or half-tracks were burning in ruby and contradictory black.

One of the fires suddenly turned to the same distant blue as the sky. The vehicle inside of it disappeared in the flash, seeming to shrink inside of some gateway the fire had opened rather than being consumed by it.

Aden counted the seconds between the detonation and the sound. It matched his estimation of the distance between them. After all, it had been the death of something from his own world.

He followed the ascending pillar of colorless fire back up to the island. The castle's beauty hypnotized him as he walked. Despite the mental defenses he tried to erect against it, for the mountain garden had shown him how vulnerable he remained to such things, he still found himself irresistibly drawn; the significance of the burning tanks below nearly erased by their graceless deaths.

Richly dressed figures moved unconcernedly along its towers and parapets, reminding him of the river trireme, occasionally gesturing or playing musical instruments whose sound reached him instantly or not at all. Aside from the burning units, there was little activity on the ridgeline, just the revolving dish antennas and ship aerials nodding to the wind. Two or three men wandered around the damaged tanks.

The sky was growing around them, progressively reducing the castle's enchantment to dimensions that fit inside Llwyellen Functions.

The tanks are only watching, Aden thought, and recalled the galleries of Joust Mountain, Kells and Dance, and how they had held their fire while thousands were incinerated for fear that their own actions might distort or contaminate their readings.

Why was the castle fighting at all? Surely its seigneur knew what had happened and why. But, Aden thought as he kept moving toward the ridgeline, if he had known, then he would have necessarily understood his own art, and the despair which had engulfed the kingdoms would have driven him to self-annihilation. Perhaps that was what he was now attempting.

He was less than a hundred meters away when a tank in the center of the line probed the castle's walls with a burst of rocket fire. There was no immediate effect. The gunner paused, probably changing magazines, and then tried again. This time the color that erupted where the round struck was that of the sky, the same that had consumed the other tank. Despite the angle, Aden could make out cracks and fissures spreading outward from the point of impact along the walls' marble facing.

Responding to this success, four other tanks and two half-tracks joined in with similar fire. The rockets left the faceted turrets cleanly and the vaporous trails of their flight remained taut in the still air, except near the walls, where the blast concussions smudged them.

They chipped patiently at the castle, tearing away filigrees of marble and sheets of gold leaf. They were not simply rockets. Aden knew that if he had the Office's eye again, he could have seen the projectiles striking the castle in every dimension and plane it existed in, crushing its beauties into formless, undifferentiated molecular pulp.

The people on the walls became more agitated, their gestures

115

wilder and less assured. One shot blasted a bridge of spider glass from under a running figure. She fell but evaporated before reaching the ground.

He was growing sick and did not know why. It was like the sicknesses he had felt each time he left Gedwyn. It grew stronger. If only the tanks and the castle would leave, both of them. Let the tanks go on with their explorations and let the mountain drift on its mage-wind for the few years left to it.

The Office's gun was in his right hand. The grip hummed like a captive insect as its circuitries changed and modified the composition of its ammunition. The wires under his scalp were hurting again, feeding undecipherable impulses into empty connectors around his left eye socket. For the first time he wondered if the secrets the eye had observed were still inscribed on the individual atoms of the melted spheres, garbled, confused but possibly retaining a singular logic.

It was a double-action automatic that could be cocked and fired with one hand. He raised the gun to eye level. One of the men who had been working around a burning tank saw him and shouted. His voice was lost in the rocket fire and crack of splitting masonry.

He started running toward Aden, looking back over his shoulder at the floating castle. Fires were beginning in its courtyards and the island itself tilted strangely on its axis. Fragments of the bolt that crushed the lead tank hit the man as he ran, turning him to the color of the sky and then to white ash.

Aden's gun fired at the same time. The gun barely moved as pistons the diameter of human hair jumped backward along its hexagonal barrel to absorb the recoil. The safety was on, and his right index finger was resting against the outside of the trigger guard.

The weapon had been pointed at a tank that was not firing, but which had been watching with its antenna arrays. He could not see the bullet hit, but one of the vehicle's slab antennas abruptly stopped rotating. As the gun intended, for it adjusted its ammunition to conform to the nature of its target, the communicative chain was broken; Aden saw this in the suddenly erratic rhythms of the other antennas.

This could not be right, he thought wildly. The gun fired again, hitting an identical antenna on the tank immediately behind the first. "This is not my work!" he said aloud to the tanks. "My ideas aren't that . . ." The gun fired a third time, and the untouched antennas jumped and spun as if they were frightened birds. Some twisted around to regard him with nervous intensity while others wavered between him, the castle and targets he could not see.

Light came arching down from the keep, striking a tank and turning it to ice. The other units responded with ferocious bursts of rocket fire, but only half of the shells hit and a third of those detonated. Trumpets and drums sang out from the castle, at once strident and fearful; they were pitched too high and often broke and faltered in the middle of calls that needed piercing clarity. Flags ran up and down the towers without apparent purpose.

Aden holstered the gun, his hands shaking with fear and uncertainty as if he expected it to forcibly resist. It hummed against his chest in the same frequency as the wires of his cranial net. He backed away, first cautiously and then at a run, running as the soldier had, looking back frantically at the continuing exchange of fire.

His sense of distance vanished in his panic. The shock of his knees locking too far above the ground drove up through his frame. He was strong and practiced in the uses and limitations of his mutilations, but there was too much surrounding him here. He had never seen the two forces actually joined in combat, reducing each other to powder, each force imprisoned by the ground on which they had to stand to strike across their divergent universes. He had lived all his life in a borderland wide enough for the Office to cultivate its extravagant paradoxes and contradictions. There was nothing but an interface around him, the two realities jammed up against one another, drooling maniacally and blindly into each other's universes with no room left for him at all. There had to be room, he was shouting to himself.

Both sides were desperately squandering their powers when he looked again. The island descended until it almost touched the earth. It tilted and spun with the same irregular rhythm of the antennas. Strangely lighted shafts traced outward from the castle. They ripped into the line of torn and burning vehicles, destroying some but failing to visibly affect others. Some of the shafts struck outward, cutting long, smoking furrows in the thick prairie grass and setting it afire; other lanced upward toward the zenith, trying to wound the sky.

The shooting by the surviving tanks became equally erratic. Some of the projectiles slammed into other vehicles while others missed hitting anything, detonating kilometers away on the prairie or rising upward like star shells, casting shadows down into the castle's interior.

The sounds that reached Aden over the pistoning of his own heart were like the screechings of fatigued metal pulling itself apart under impossible stress.

Aden stopped when he heard this and turned to watch the underside of the island dig into the ground. It tilted forward, digging a trench toward the tanks. He could see into the courtyards and gardens inside the walls. The perspective momentarily disoriented him for it seemed as if he was looking down on the castle from some altitude, rather than standing on the ground. It was the same illusion that the sky and the distant, sloping horizon played upon him when he first saw the island.

The building cracked apart and slid from its foundation; then the island itself dropped down onto the vehicles. There was the blue light again, an oval splash of sky reaching down into the earth, ignoring the boundaries of the horizon, spreading outward to where Aden was, threatening to cut the ground from under him and plunge him into a gulf of metal-colored sunlight, without limit or definition.

The concussion caught him around the hips and in the small of his back and lifted him with scornful gentleness. It carried him upward, through the sky and then toward a growing circle of

blackness that he entered. Within it there was no sound or movement but the distant humming of the wires inside his skull and
the Office's gun puzzling over this new environment, postulating
what sort of enemies might live within it.

Hovercraft were like ships, Etridge was fond of pointing out.
They answered their helms slowly and with an imprecision that
demanded a practiced hand at the wheel. They had to be sailed
over the earth. Their routes of passage had to be carefully
planned for inclination, surface integrity and clearance between
landmarks. All that, at sixty-five kilometers an hour. A properly
handled two hundred tonner could be an impressive sight, racing
across a foreign plain, the ground beneath it turning to dust as if
it had been ignited, antennas and gun turrets regarding the passing landscape with disconcerting stability.

Stamp was glad at this moment that Etridge had selected him
as his aide, if only to have been on the hoverships and not the
tanks. But he still would have felt more comfortable if they were
following along with their treads and wheels and jouncing antennas. Etridge had been told by Lake Gilbert that they had been
wiped out, and had been asked what the hell they were doing out
there in the first place. Etridge replied, as he had before, that in
view of sharply decreased enemy activity, a reconnaissance in
force was justified. But so far into his lands? Lake Gilbert
persisted. Etridge played with the radio spectrums so that it appeared that his position was nine hundred kilometers west of
where they actually were.

The lack of solid information as to the column's destruction
pleased Stamp, as did Etridge's scarcely concealed anger with it.
He noted how the veins and muscles stood out from the old
man's neck and how the planes of his face jerked from calm for
the benefit of the crew, to repressed fury as he again reviewed
the readout tapes and the last communications with the column.

"The men of power still seem to be around in some force."

"And ability." Etridge balled up a sheaf of papers and threw it
into a corner. The hoverships were traversing a long canyon

floor and they bucked and rocked as the helmsmen braked with their engines and drag skids.

"We may not be so far along as we thought."

"We are. The tanks had that, whatever that fairy-tale contraption was, blocked and halfway understood. It should have been turned into dust."

"It was," Stamp mentioned gratuitously.

"So were our own people, goddamnit! There was no reason for it." Etridge picked up another sheet of printout. "No, that's not right. There are reasons. They just look like questions right now. Here." He held the sheet under Stamp's chin and then snatched it back. "Multiple readings, 'jokers' we called them before Thorn River, showing up just when the column signaled that they'd figured out the castle's power."

"Another mystery, another manifestation of that magician's way of doing things that they couldn't analyze before it got them. *We* didn't see the power of that fire-beast when it came in. It was even hidden from the wind ships."

Anderton came up to the console and braced himself. "Pardon me, sir, the readings aren't completely unknown. If you'll look along the third and fifth lines you'll see they're identical with the ones we picked up a few weeks ago, when we asked Lake Gilbert about the Special Office files."

Etridge's eyes turned inward. "You're sure?"

"Just about. Not only the same sort of power indications, but maybe the same person or entity."

"All right. That could make sense. Tell Lake Gilbert that . . ."—seeing Anderton's question—"tell them again that we have got to have access to their files."

"If we gave them the reason," Stamp ventured carefully, "wouldn't that indicate just where *we* are and what we are really doing?"

"But we are not here, Stamp. We're just making a borderland reconnaissance as standing orders and my rank as director of Joust Mountain both obligate me to do."

"Then it seems we will be playing the game the Office used to."

"The game was never played because that player never existed." Etridge's voice showed he was forcibly suppressing the destruction of the tank columns and the loss of the castle's mysteries. He rubbed his jaw lightly. "But if we are doing that, where do you think it will take us?"

"To victory!" Anderton replied mechanically, though the question had been directed to Stamp.

They traveled beyond the range of the wind ships. That was another advantage of the hovercraft. Although they were restricted to relatively flat surfaces and gentle gradients, their tremendous lifting capacity allowed them to carry the shielding necessary for fusion motors.

Large animals of reassuringly non-magical varieties were unexpectedly plentiful with the warming weather, so food was no problem.

Stamp had hoped that the distance they put between themselves and home might have eroded morale and forced Etridge to turn back. Instead the men seemed to draw closer to Etridge. The lack of any other authority from home gave his fanaticism space in which to grow and acquire the appeal that Heisner had found so terrible.

The frequency of enchanted ruins had obligingly increased as they moved farther into the kingdoms. At each one, they stopped and studied until they had understood the details of its construction and the heritage of the man of power it had been built to honor or protect or entomb.

There were small engagements too, but nothing like the fire-minotaur and the dead cavalry they had encountered at the first village. Only forlorn and solitary hydras, poisoned wells, badgering homuncului the size and shape of bats, all hideous little dreams that the ships' computers easily handled.

They lost no more than one or two men to each of these irritations. Stamp perversely speculated as to whether Etridge was not also studying their deaths as well as those of the monsters that had inflicted them.

They were within two days of the Holy City. The land around them was covered by a magnificent forest of oak and ironwood trees. Many of the boles on the trees had been laboriously carved or had naturally grown into semi-human masks. They had to move slowly, while the laser guns of the lead ship cut an avenue for them. Stamp watched the faces drift by as they passed, many of them charred and smoking from the light, and they regarded him with murderously tranquil eyes.

Anderton explained that the trees were endowed with unusual phototropic tendencies. The carvings were also the result of gene mutation and when the sensitized bole-endings picked up side flashes from the lasers, they naturally followed. There really was movement and apparent changes of expression, but it was the mindless reaction of cells to ordinary occurrences.

Against this, Stamp pointed out the extraordinary naturalness of the faces in the way they moved and narrowed their eye-carvings, tightening the bark around the skulls that might have been carved underneath them. Anderton replied, "suggestion," and offered to show him the psychological gradients to prove it.

In any event, the gunner continued, there was no need to worry. Morgan, the life-analysis man, had found evidence of rapid gene deterioration. The power that had forced the trees into their simulation of watching, perhaps as an elaborate mockery of the masses of antennas that surrounded the cities of their own world, was located in the Holy City, and it was failing. Soon the forest would be like any other and Anderton remarked that he might like to come back when he retired from the Border Command and build a house from the fine, sturdy trunks.

The lasers burned away the forest for a radius of seven hundred meters when they set down that night. Etridge ordered that their full power be shunted into the guns once the lift engines were shut down, and they paved the cleared ground with a seamless sheet of green glass five centimeters thick.

Their losses had demanded that the crews spread themselves more thinly than they would have liked. It was therefore easy for Stamp to enter the ship's auxiliary radio cabin unnoticed. He shut and dogged the door behind him and sat down at the console.

Why, he asked himself a dozen times before concluding that there was no answer, did he out of all the survivors, have the need to cling to the ruins of magic. Certainly Etridge's abilities of command had been sufficiently demonstrated; why then did he further judge the nature of the mission that the man had undertaken.

The man did not even give him the comfort of reprimand or rebuke; there were only his opaque syllogisms, each one of which made Stamp feel like he was being shoved along more and more certainly by the velocity of the man's obsession.

He thought he had felt the air of the forest cutting more deeply into his heart as Etridge guided them along, peeling the stabilities of the regular services from his memories with the same reductivism that he used to shatter the remnants of magic. His family, his ambitions, dead lovers, the peace his home had established against the encircling violence of the war, they had all been eroded by Etridge, their definitions erased by the course and direction he had chosen for the ships.

Stamp shook himself and opened the appropriate channels. He left the "voice" switch off; video readout would be more discreet.

He slowly typed his inquiries and accusations, and when the screen in front of him was filled with luminous green letters, pressed the "transmit" button. The information went out in two block transmissions of a fifth of a second each to Lake Gilbert; identification, location, force, personnel, course, casualties, destination, the code for suspected incompetence of command.

Stamp received no immediate response and repeated the message. On the third try, Lake Gilbert answered by correcting all of his information. They were, Lake Gilbert silently, unctuously informed him, thirteen hundred and seventy kilometers northwest of his reported position; they had sustained only two casualties due to enemy action; one tank and three half-tracks remained with them; their line of travel roughly paralleled the fortress line between Kells, Joust Mountain, Dance and First Valley. The reconnaissance was, Lake Gilbert trusted, going well but it reminded the sender to refrain from aggressive activities against the enemy or any deep penetrations into his territory until the strategic parameters of the war had clarified. Interference with their operation by Special Office was impossible in that no such organization had ever existed.

Finally, reports of incompetence, unless sent from a "recognized combat area" were ineffective if not confirmed by a medical officer. Since both their doctors had been killed, Stamp left this item out of each of his three succeeding attempts at attracting Lake Gilbert's attention. Each time, he encountered the same response. He thought of opening voice channels and arguing with whoever was on the other end of the transmission, but decided against it since it was probably a machine.

The words from the last reply stayed on the screen for a minute and then erased themselves. He could hear only the ventilators. Television monitors on the panels above his head reported the flat gleam of moonlight on the sentry tripods around the ships; their beacon lights shone an alternating blue and orange.

The faces on the trees were gone and lost now. There were just the beacons and the white, silent bulk of the other hovercraft on the aft monitor screens. Even at rest, the ship implied motion, silent and imperial across a night paved with glass made by laser cannons. In his frustration and loneliness, he imagined the faces of all the creatures of magic upturned and staring under the surface of the glass road, acting as its foundation, absorbing the shocks of passage that began with the whispering of the high wind ships, descended through the captive storms of the hovercraft, and led, eventually, to the grinding of tank treads and hobnailed boots. They would scar the surface of the glass road, until those who marched upon it could no longer see down into all the lost myths crushed underneath, and they, in turn, were spared the sight of their enemy's triumph and rightness.

He thought, that is happening now, and I find it progressively more difficult to preserve whatever dreams I might have had about this magic. Since the raising of the fire-minotaur, I have seen nothing to indicate that there is anything more than parlor tricks left, dragons pulled from silk hats, as Etridge put it. They were more real when I looked at them through the radio telescopes at Joust Mountain, or read of their barbarities on commemorative plaques at Thorn River and Heartbreak Ridge.

"You see the logic of it?" Etridge had come into the room behind him. Stamp felt broken and far away enough to mask any surprise.

"I see the necessity of it, even for myself," Stamp answered after a while, with some bitterness staining his words. Etridge did not dispute it.

From the hills above the Holy City, Aden could see a line of blue gray along the southeastern horizon: the ocean was coming back. Soon the place would be known as Cape St. Vincent again. The ocean would advance and drown the palaces and pavilions the magicians had built on the dry seabed as evidence of their power.

He had watched the City for two days, sitting in the same place, trying to fit the patterns of its overgrown gardens and rubble-choked streets into his memories. Three and a half million people had lived there, ruled and overawed by two hundred and seventy men of power and a horde of lesser magicians, monks, acolytes, apprentice sorcerers.

Now only occasional figures moved across the blasted plazas. Pegasuses in tattered liveries, their wings the color of canvas, wandered out of the City and came close enough for him to identify them. Packs of wild dogs harried those that could no longer fly, easily encircling two or three at a time and destroying them.

As he watched, the line of the ocean thickened at the edge of the world, though that could be an illusion brought on by the setting sun. Dark specks that were probably islands seemed to move and acquired the silhouettes of battle cruisers and aircraft carriers.

The 18x scope sight was fitted into the front of his holster. Aden removed it and locked it onto the barrel, just forward of the action's lug pivot. He reversed the holster and clipped its narrow end to the butt to form a shoulder stock.

The scope perceived the City, as it had Gedwyn, in eight of the parallel spectrums. It reviewed each one in turn, progressing outward from normal, visible light, revealing the completeness of the City's desertion. The gun's magazine vibrated in a different harmonic with each filtering system the scope used.

The core of the City retained hints of beauty and power. Aden recognized the domed temple where he had found the unicorn and its attendant and where his eye had been taken from him. The scope revealed successive dimensions of beauty as it interrogated the temple's minarets and vast mosaics, found its alabaster windows unbroken and its bronze doors locked and awaiting the arrival of men with powers sufficient to open them.

The fountain was there too. There was no water coming from it, but the dolphins and seraphim gushed luminous scarlet and turquoise plasmas that poured over the fountain's rim and across the plaza with the insubstantiality of clouds.

The quarter where Donchak's house had been was a tumble of gutted shells, freestanding walls and piles of masonry. There were also traces of sorcerous power left in that area of the City, but it was mostly of the minor sort, orphaned homunculi, incantations stopped in mid-casting, one demon assassin, exhausted by the vengeance locked in his heart, hunting a man who had died by his own choice months before.

The wires woven into his head sang as they had for the past two days. Instead of the intermittent monotone he had grown used to, Aden read another level into their pain. Perhaps it was the unicorn that was reaching out to him; he had not admitted to that possibility before. Perhaps it had used the eye in the way that he could have, had he had the time and the peace, had he not worked in the interests of his world, had he not fallen in love with someone from the other.

He rubbed his hand against the leather patch, testing the emptiness behind it and the carved ridges of the perpetually open eye on its front. It was conceivable that the Office had rigged the patch for perception and transmission without telling him. The doctor-machine had seemed pleased when he had shown it to him, just before he left for the Taritan Valley. But, even if this was true, the motives of a mythic organization embarked on missions consisting principally of self-deception could hardly matter to a man in his situation.

That situation being one of treason. The classical offense against the deities, someone had pointed out to him, was vanity, hubris. But there were no gods left to offend in the world, only nations, and the highest attainable sin was therefore treason. In distracting the tanks and possibly allowing the castle to escape into death, he had committed the first treasonous act in the kingdoms of magic, where emulation of the godhead had formerly been the worst a man, commoner or magician, could aspire to.

I affirm my world, even when I act against it to preserve magic against transmutation into numbers and equations. Good; that implied that there was still some room left between the two worlds for him to function in.

The land to the south of the City, between the flattened hills and the ocean, was thick forest. Aden examined it through the scope sight, noting the broken towers of obsidian and tourmaline that rose through the green cover. Strangely colored birds the size of men and dressed in armor soared above the land, darting back and forth above the forest to catch the thermal currents rising from its borders with the hills.

There were sourceless flashes of light too, that suddenly illuminated irregular patches of the woods, rushed through the various spectrums and then faded. The explosions or signals were rarely accompanied by any sound, but he could usually pick out wisps of smoke and plasma rising lazily from their general location. One such area appeared to be at the end of a dark, twisting avenue that had been cut through the forest. It had not been there the night before.

Aden examined it through the scope. The path followed the contours of the land, holding to implied, geometrically precise curves and parabolas as it wound along the ancient drainage and rills.

There were other blast traces scattered through the forest. They marked the destruction of isolated pockets of magic and power and the trees had grown thickly over where they had been. They had imploded upon themselves and left nothing behind. The avenue was different; it was rich in heavy particle radiations and the peculiar resonances which exotic alloys often touched off in adjoining spectrums.

The vehicles were at the end of the road. They were fast and well armed. The army of occupation. Aden imagined the land collapsing in on itself, rushing to surround and smother the last few secrets it held—not quickly enough.

The gun murmured to him, sentient, probing the asylum death offered the men of power and their works from the pursuit of the Border Command. Death remained special and singular, but the war had merged it with love and loyalty and hatred and all other mysteries. Aden could think of nothing which could truly differentiate death from the rest of them, aside from the fact that it had been the first and was now the last. There was nothing which showed it to be beyond the reach of the men in the hovercraft and those that would follow, any more than the other mysteries had been.

Aden dropped the gun onto his crossed legs and found himself shivering despite the warmth of the air. He ran the gun's barrel along his sleeve, absently tracing the veins and scars and lines left from the skin grafts and emplacement of wires.

He should feel differently. This was the end of the war. Instead he felt as deserted as the City, spoken to only by buried scar tissue and memories of unicorns more distant than that of the one woman he had been able to love. Is this not, he asked the gun, how all old men feel? Then, knowing that he had always felt that way, he further considered that the Office had always been old, too.

As the air darkened, crystallized tree stumps reflected the first ship's laser cannons. Around it, the fires of the dying kingdoms incinerated the tombs of mages, fertilizing the land with their transmuting ashes, luring vines and seedlings into the charred clearings to hide their shame and defeat.

Aden stayed on the rock outcropping for most of that night. The two ships had settled to the ground just after dusk. Their clearing of a wide security perimeter would have blinded him if the gunsight had not automatically shifted its filters.

Blue and orange monitor light marked sentry guns posted around the encampment. A complete darkness reached more than three kilometers beyond them into the forest. After that border, the forest resumed its decay, exploding quietly and burning away or dumbly stalking enemies who had made themselves invincible.

Dragons sometimes roared out, seeking the bidding of vanished masters. Enormous blocks of stone that had been welded into towers and redoubts by ineffable forces, broke apart and fell into moats filled with the glowing skeletons of ichthyosaurs.

The gun could not hear this, it could only see. Aden lay against a rock with cabalistic inscriptions chiseled above his head and drifted from the forest's night to his own, then out to the night that was demarcated by the orange and blue beacons. At some intervals he thought he could hear the ocean, at others Gedwyn's voice.

He was sure the eye was still in the unicorn, though much had changed in the world since he had left the hospital. This, despite the fact that it was much more reasonable to presume that the unicorn was gone and the eye simply remained along the floor of the cathedral's nave, staring fixedly at the high altar, reporting the monthly accumulations of dust on the chalices and sacred books to the Special Office.

It will be there, he thought. Its image, hard and glistening, swam through the dark interior of his eye socket, immune to the understanding of whatever devices the men in the forest had brought with them.

He saw the unicorn again, the purest embodiment of legend and mystery, moving incomprehensibly through the world, as remote and present as dreams. Ah, he thought, the Special Office's heart may be at one with it. He conceived of the single creature as the underground, guerrilla army of the defeated kingdoms. It would be possible to live in a world where such forces still operated, and it would be necessary for the Special Office to return to protect it.

All through the night, the gun had whispered to itself, conversing with Aden through the wires under his skin, or with the Office over the nonexistent frequencies to Lake Gilbert.

Etridge nodded to Anderton. "All right. What are they saying?"

"The upper three traces"—the other man underlined some readings on an oscilloscope with his light pencil—"are using the old Special Office channels. Even the same scramble techniques." Anderton referred to an open notebook with tan and brittle pages. "Now, this one, you can see, is very different. It extends laterally through several spectrums and trails off into places I'd say exist only in a theoretic sense."

"Our unicorn?"

"Its eye, at least. See the similarities in its wave patterns with those of the first two transmissions?"

Etridge did not, but he nodded anyway. "Any directions on them?"

"The first and the third are directed mainly to Lake Gilbert, and the second one is a responding signal."

"You say, mainly."

Anderton hid his embarrassment behind his radiation scars. "Ah, they also contain secondary signals directed toward us."

"Us?" Etridge brought his face closer to the scope. "That might fit in. The Office could hardly resist speaking to one side of its world without hinting to the other that something was going on. Balance. They hold balance very dearly, you know."

"Sir?" Anderton had been concentrating on getting more definition on the signals, but they remained unfocused.

Instantly, all of the screens across the panel were filled with raging light. Anderton started in his chair and braced his hands against the console as if the luminescence carried a physical impact.

Etridge jerked back too, the surfaces of his face closing shut like the armor of the hovercraft. Watch personnel left their stations and nervously circled the room to get a better look.

This was in silence. Over it, Etridge said: "Would that be our unicorn, Mr. Anderton?"

"Yes sir," he whispered through the colors, touching one or two dials to confirm his own words.

"Does he still address us?"

"It's the eye, the eye, sir. It can't be the creature because it has no power without its master."

"No more than the Office which built the eye in the first place." Colors counter-played inside the bridge, drowning the grids and Kessler-graphs in their swirling torrents. Etridge was dressed in his black uniform, standing in the middle of it. His clothes swallowed the colors, and the metallic whiteness of his skin reflected away everything but an occasional flicker of scarlet.

Obscurely terrified by the colors' violent beauty, Anderton stood up and backed away from his scopes and closer to Etridge's rigidly held blackness. The other men, including Stamp, did the same.

The ship's computers whirred in their cabinets, digesting the flood of information they perceived, searching their accumulated records with measured desperation until an appropriate analogue was found for a particular unknown, the resultant hypothesis tested and proven into a postulate.

"Does it, the unicorn—is *that* what it's seeing too?" Tidal rushes of brilliance beat against scope frames that had patent numbers and manufacturers' plaques riveted to them, threatening to burst out into the room.

"Could the . . . ?"

"That is what the Special Office had been watching? Ah, god." Anderton, crooning low, his voice human and unrelated to his own machines for the first time in months. The man sagged within his uniform; his wide shoulders bent, his pity and astonishment crowded the fear from his joints and let him sit down and cover his eyes.

Etridge said nothing at all. He had established a circle of tired, cynical tranquillity around him. The lights had jolted him at first, but his clothes and skin protected him. All the imponderable beauties of the world, he hinted simply by standing there with his hands clasped behind him, staring straight into the scopes, could be shown to be no more, and possibly less than the sum of their component parts. Man, granted his peculiar affliction of mortality, honed and sharpened through his ages of disappointment, would annihilate first the wonders of magic and then the larger mysteries of death and the soul. Beyond that, god might be discovered, cowering in the tumbled ruin of his own failed creation, his measure taken, and the universe shown to be outside of his control. And then, even that would be studied and broken. They would be alone, safe, no longer menaced by mystery and the anxiety of wondering, all the reasons for heartbreak contained and quantified.

That was why Etridge had frightened Stamp; but he had never seen what had driven the man. Isolated by the limits of Anderton's scopes, the colors of the unicorn's perceptions were still worse than any cold and lonely end Etridge might lead them to.

The alienness of what the scopes contained battered him, and set up a reaction that drove him toward Etridge to share his protective despair. The war, Stamp realized, was not nearly over. A specific enemy may have been defeated or driven off, but his weapons remained to be picked up by whatever random god or madman might stumble upon them.

Stamp glanced around the bridge. The colors made the forward part of the room burn with a thousand different fires, and each one was squared and then cubed by each of the succeeding spectrums in which it burned.

Etridge stepped back to Anderton's station. He looked down

the rows of screens and then adjusted filter dials, timidly at first and then with more decision.

The computers assisted with more precisely defined parameters. The colors compressed and withdrew from the borders of the screens; they began to fit within their intended limits on the Kessler-graphs. As though pleased with their success, the computers' electric murmuring eased; overload lights switched from red back into blue. The patterns continued to resolve themselves until, while they retained their stunning beauty, they were comprehensible within the experience of men. They no longer threatened the mind but only the heart, and that could be controlled.

"The eye remains," Etridge mentioned needlessly when the colors had gone, and everyone nodded as if he had suddenly made it true. "The unicorn can still see with it, and the Office is still looking."

"Are we undetected?"—Stamp.

Etridge referred to banks of dials on the right side of the cabin. "No. There seem to be various source detections, both reflective from that little display you just saw, and crude spectrum ranging from the highlands to the northwest of us." Anderton nodded in confirmation.

"Target?" Anderton asked upon finding his voice. He stepped back to his position and ran his hand along the rows of toggle switches. Stamp heard the turrets on the hovercraft's topsides moving.

"Not yet." Etridge waved him away and the turrets quieted. "We'll be in there tomorrow. We don't want to be blowing up our own people." He looked at Stamp. "The Office, you know."

"It is our enemy, too?" Stamp asked from far away.

"Not yet," Etridge repeated.

Aden's campfire had burned through the night in three of the nearest spectrums, excluding that of visible light. Discolored leaves and twigs of certain herbs smoldered in the semicircle of rocks. He stamped it out, and made the appropriate gestures through the proper spectrums to fully extinguish it.

It will be good to see again. He looked to the horizon, to the advancing ocean, and chuckled at his pun.

Aden rose, unclipped the scope from the holster and sighted down into the forest. Fountains of infrared light poured upward from the near end of the avenue as the hoverships warmed up their engines. The dawn sun raked across the treetops, shattering a tower of stained glass and another of yellow diamond with the weight of its light.

He chose a shallow drainage which would shield him from unassisted observation and carefully followed it. After half an hour, he encountered a cyclops lying across the trail. From the smell, the thing had been dead for some time, and there was a great scattering of bones and pieces of weapons around it.

The sun moved up, warming the segmented carcass inside its rusting armor. Ants crawled across the empty eye socket of the monster and gnawed at the strands of tendon that locked its hand around a mace.

Aden shifted and noted a movement on the left. He continued turning, more slowly, and saw a dwarf sitting on a rock above him. He was playing noiselessly on a mahogany flute, addressing his songs to the dead cyclops and then to the other bodies around it. He paused and bowed toward each one in turn. By following his gesturing, Aden spotted more and more corpses on either side of the gully until he estimated their numbers in the hundreds.

Aden's surprise quieted. He remembered that it was often the custom of the men of power to commemorate their victories, and sometimes their defeats if they had been at the hand of some particularly worthy foe, with the presence of such a player. Being made of magic, they lived and sang by their graveyards until a newer battle erased them or the power that conjured them was itself erased.

Aden walked through the bodies. The flute player had eyes made of stone and took no notice of him. He passed close to the miniature human, bent near to him and heard a tune he thought he recognized from years ago. If he had the eye back he could have seen into the other spectrums where the song was being played and learn the true meaning of the battle.

The drainage opened onto the plain before the City. He passed by the scenes of other encounters, each without apparent reason or cause but all having been fought only between the adherents of magic. There were no shell casings, no spent cartridges and no chemical residues that the gunsight could discover to show that his world had had a hand in any of them. He found only more dismembered myths of the sort that carpeted the dry lake in front of Joust Mountain after the great battle there, swords engraved with still glowing runes and baroque mottoes written with dragons' blood on the ground beside dead giants.

Each successive battle site had its attendant watcher. They were mostly built along human lines but were invariably dwarfs or stunted, as if their diminished statures could exaggerate the importance of an engagement by contrast. Some played flutes like the first he had seen, while others strummed lyres carved from rosewood and inlaid with pearl, monotonously beat animal skin drums with curved talons dangling over their rims, or just sang wordlessly.

Aden ventured up along the slope of the hill on his left as far as he dared without chancing discovery by the hovercraft and found more of the same. The land was pockmarked with the remains of small, bitterly contested fights, spreading in a rough arc around the walls of the City. There were no great lines which would have indicated the maneuvering of organized companies toward any goal. It was more as if the magicians had emptied all the City's grotesques out onto the foothills, told them the slurs their brothers had committed against their masters' names, and set them upon each other until all were dead.

The gunsight showed that the dead had many different kinds of magic clinging to them, but the memorialists were formed from a single power. The rhyme and measure of their songs, when one could hear them, indicated a common basis.

A sea gull screeched in the air above Aden. It orbited him for a minute and then flew off, back to its ocean to feed on garbage from his world's approaching navies.

Magic, defeated by the examinations of his world, might have sought to affirm its own existence by turning upon itself. The men of power had continued their internecine wars even as they prosecuted their larger offensives against rationality, so it was not inconceivable that their servants had attacked each other as their masters sickened and died. They must have been the last, and the unicorn, alone but for its own servitors, may have created the dwarfs to bear witness to their struggles.

Aden reached the foundations of the road he had left the City on. He was in the open now but at the same elevation on which the hovercraft must approach; the forest would hide him. Steles and pylons, many discolored and snapped in half, bordered it. Everywhere, he conceived, there was commemoration and memorial, projections of thought and alien sentiment that reached through time to connect the observer to the powers that had caused them.

There would be no such monuments raised by the people he had seen last night. They will regard them as signposts whose existences will taunt them and draw them farther along. The unicorn would be sought out for the same reasons.

Aden walked more quickly. Last night he had put together reasons for fearing the arrival of the men. Now he realized that he might be one of them. Though he sought only the eye that had once been his, he was still here. He had used weapons of his own world, the gun and his knowledge of the tank column's analytic web, in destroying both it and the fairy castle.

A hollick the size of a ferret scuttled across the road in front of him. The gun was in his hand instantly. He tracked it until it disappeared into a crumbling tomb on the left.

The gun hummed irritably in his hand. He pointed it to the southeast, to where the forest came closest to the City's walls. High plumes of plasma jetted into the air behind peacock fans of questing radiation. The ships are looking, he whispered to the gun, they are deciphering everything, every deserted altar, corpse, creature, rune and scrap of magical rubbish left behind.

Aden was sweating. His palms glistened when he held them open, and for a moment he feared that their increased conductance would distort the gun's perceptions.

"The old coastline followed this elevation, here." Bock traced a line with his finger. His hands were small and delicate, as was his body, and that was permissible for a cartographer. He had been distrusted by rear echelon people because he had shown some fascination with the nature of the enemy in the way he decorated his maps with fanciful castles and mythic bestiaries. For the same reasons, Etridge valued his presence and his loyalty. "Assuming a steady rate of advance, the ocean should be back to its original borders in four years. After that, I would think intensive dredging can have the harbors ready for deep water traffic in three more."

"Very good, after seven hundred years."

"Better than good," Bock warmed to the subject. "These people never seem to have touched the land. Bauxite, rare earths, pitchblende so rich I'd think that's what makes parts of this country glow at night, copper lodes you hardly need to refine. And all that gold and silver and lapis lazuli they conjured up out of mud is transmuting back into stable nitrogen and phosphorus compounds. The land'll be a garden. It'll be like coming to a new country." Bock looked out the ship's windscreen, fitting his personal mythologies into degrees of latitude and longitude, feeling the earth whole again between his compass and dividers.

They were wrong about the man. He's ours, just infatuated with their stage dressings; it's part of growing up on one's way to attack the godhead. Etridge smiled and Bock thought it was to share his delight in the new land.

"Sir!" the man at the wheel called out to Etridge. "The City!" The trees thinned out as they came onto the plain around the City's walls.

Etridge pushed his hand forward and the engines accelerated in response, blurring the late summer grasses beneath them.

The windows cleared to show the City, long quays and stumps

of cranes fronting the skyline of dissolving minarets. Stamp had a notebook open and recited the names of the structures he matched up with old photographs or with the multi-spectrum pictures the unicorn's eye had sent back.

Curving roads faced with marble intersected their path. Grass and weeds had pushed between the paving blocks and were already splitting some of them in two. Piles of skeletons could be observed on either side of the ships; each one had a small creature playing a flute or lyre or other instrument standing beside it. Stamp saw them raise their heads from their playing and stare at the approaching ships.

As they sailed by the players dropped their instruments and expressions of sadness crossed their remotely human faces. Stamp knew the white sides of the hovercraft retained their gleam and polish and speculated as to whether it was the ships or the creatures' own reflections which caused them to look that way.

Anderton reported that the players held no power other than that which sustained their lives; they posed no overt threat. The source of the power itself was identified and traced to the City. Anderton requested permission to hit one of them, but Etridge said it would hardly be worth the trouble.

The City's dimensions sharpened as they approached. The port of Cape St. Vincent had been absorbed by an incredible mass of palaces, guild halls, temples, private fortresses, circuses and baths. They had all seen the reconnaissance photos and the architects' elevations posted for a hundred meters along the main corridors of Joust Mountain. But they had not been prepared for this. Even Etridge. He judged that the City was already in an advanced state of decay. What could its beauty have been like five or twenty years ago? It was possible, he admitted to himself, that the force of the City's splendor alone could have stopped our missiles in mid-flight and smothered the blast of their warheads.

That was what the Special Office had dealt with every day for three hundred years.

"Ever seen colors like that? Not like last night, no, but look, look . . ."

"Jeez, that dome, to the left of those three towers. You have that map?"

"*H* Town itself. I'd never thought I'd get to see it standing up or even want to."

"Ten, possibly fifteen kilometers."

"Imagine the effort that went into that. Must have taken at least . . ."

The voices rose over the engines.

"And the lot of it falling to pieces like wet paper," Etridge said loudly. "Look at them." He pointed out at the gaping memorialists. "Look how much in love they were with their own power and now with their own death. They were in love with themselves, so deeply they acknowledged nothing else." The ships passed on either side of a tangle of skeletons with its attendant player, and the blast from their supporting air cushions scattered them like jackstraws.

The conversation returned to the normal subjects of range, speed, navigation, energy analysis. Etridge pressed his hands together on the grab bar and permitted his eyes to wander away from the City. If only we were all Andertons and Bocks. He knew that if Stamp now agreed with him it was as much from unacknowledged hatred of the City and the wizards for failing as from any allegiance to him. They had proved themselves weak and vulnerable. However long their threat would linger in the world, it had shown itself capable of defeat and could therefore be feared with a righteousness that hid one's sense of divine betrayal.

Etridge wondered briefly how much of his own thoughts were motivated by loyalty to the world's way of doing things, and how much could be attributed to the wizards for having allowed themselves to be defeated and their dreams with them. Had he seen that, too, at Thorn River?

Stamp waited beside him, referring to the notebook and making corrections on the maps with a pen. Bock was seated to the right of the helmsman; his arms were braced on the control panel as he patiently took photos of their approach. A cable connected the camera to the ranging computers and made it unnecessary to constantly adjust the focus.

"Have you found an opening yet?"

The pilot gestured toward the northern end of the walls that faced them. "Gate Five."

"What did *they* call it?"

"The Teachers' Door," Stamp volunteered; his voice was flat and abstracted.

"Good. After all, we're here to learn. Aren't we, Bock?"

Bock nodded behind his camera. "All we can."

"All there is," Stamp continued in the same tone.

"Anderton. Tell the second unit to find a position up in those hills where they can see as much of the City as possible and still be in range of everything but their smallest stuff. Make sure the area is secure. If they can avoid those musicians and their pet bone heaps, they should. No souvenir hunting. And constant surveillance through all the spectrums as long as we're inside."

"How far in can we take the ship?"

Stamp flipped to an aerial photograph of the City; it was in infrared, so it had the appearance of a negative. "This avenue"—he indicated with his pen—"leads from the Door to a plaza, here. From there we can take either this street or this one into the old section of town. That's where the only real power readings are located."

"The unicorn, do you think?"

"The position is roughly the same as that of the transmission we got last night."

"The eye, too?"

Stamp shrugged. Another enemy blunder. Even he had been able to find it. A year and the poor beast had not caught on to the fact that it was still revealing itself and its master, if he was still around, to the world. "Same position, same power characteristics. Both of them running on identical lines."

Etridge found himself momentarily depressed by the other man's words. Unavoidably, he felt that *he* had taken the belief from Stamp, rather than having merely shown him how fragile and insubstantial it was. Soon, he thought, the disappointment will break up enough to allow the hatred and contempt to surface; then the desperate intoxication of the pursuit would overtake him. That was the way it had worked after Thorn River.

The other hovercraft fell behind and then glided away from them.

Their ship paralleled the City's western wall. Fragments of vast mosaics depicted the heads and limbs of unimaginable beasts, great armies of gilded warriors and the slaughter of hovercraft such as their own.

Etridge wished that the crew was speaking again, if only in astonishment at the walls. The quiet in the cabin was that of the unbeliever in the cathedral, equally awe and embarrassment, each emotion reflecting back upon the other and magnifying it. There were only a few bodies this close to the walls. There was nothing around which could dilute the size and majesty of the City with its pathetic defeat.

At least there were the engines and the sounds of the scopes and the antenna drives and computers, all of them thoroughly unimpressed with the ruins whose binding forces they had striven for years to untie.

Etridge knew that the application of certain radiant energies would instantly obliterate every mosaic that remained. Others would cause the walls themselves to collapse—which they would do of their own accord within a year. That would be incorrect. He might bury the unicorn before his ships could understand it.

The unicorn was a servant, possibly still serving its master though he had died. He had been the City's greatest magician, if the carefully edited reports of the Special Office could be believed. The lines of power that still connected him to his servant must be found and followed.

There it was. Etridge felt his energy returning. He sensed it growing in Stamp and Bock and Anderton too. Something at last to occupy the field that had been deserted for the first time in seven hundred years, something overwhelming enough to contain and animate their mortality and rage.

Carefully now, he reminded himself. This too was a spell that could be broken like all the others. He learned how to preserve it at Thorn River when thousands were incinerated while he gently probed and tapped against the skins of their destroyers. "Are we near the gate?"

"One kilometer."

"There should be an approach road. Set it down there, five hundred meters from the Door. We'll wait for the other unit to get established, and then go in tomorrow morning. Stamp and I, and two more men will be on foot. Walking speed, and try to be as careful as you can. I'm sure the museum people will want to see everything as authentically as possible."

"Tourists," Anderton snorted.

"No," Etridge said lightly. "Remember, gentlemen, we are not here. We are hundreds of kilometers to the west, exploring border lands recently vacated by our distinguished adversaries."

"I don't think Lake Gilbert cares where we might be." The desolation remained in Stamp's voice. So many things were being taken from him so quickly: the consequence of having clung to them too long.

"So much the better. We can live with their indifference. If they did want to know where we really were, I think it might be just as much to stop us as help us along." Mutinous talk, even for a commander on the edge of retirement and a continent away from his headquarters.

They drew level with the Teachers' Door, swerved to face it and then settled to the road's surface. Etridge appreciated the drama of the scene and hoped he was not overplaying it.

Anderton leaned over in his chair and touched his sleeve. "Presence on the walls, sir."

Below Aden and several hundred meters to the west, the boat-shaped hovercraft waited while an identical unit sped away toward the hills he had just come down from. The purity of their whiteness burned into his eye and made it difficult to distinguish the turrets and antenna domes that pebbled their topsides.

Still only two of them. He looked again and recognized Border Command chevrons on their vertical stabilizers. If the world had chosen to ignore the direction pointed to by the Taritan Valley, the air would have been thick with transports, wind ships and armored helicopters bringing men to bury the dead palaces under linear steel and polymeric roadbeds straight as rifle shots. Instead there were two renegade ships.

He reached the street. Withered, whitened trunks of jewel-maples in onyx planters bordered it, the skeletons of grotesque birds caught in their branches as the sparrows had been in Gedwyn's garden. Aden sat on the edge of one and tried to calm himself. He knew the City. They did not. But they had photos and maps and possibly the image that the eye, *his* eye had sent back to the Special Office. The ships could see through walls. They could probe into solid nuclear masses and listen to the sound of his breathing on the other side.

The wires under his skin were inert. Coldness occupied the empty space where the eye had been. The Special Office was absent this morning. Only its weapon remained, and its eternal humming seemed to be of the same range and frequency as the singing of the memorialists.

That parallel was too close. Both the Office and the men of power had withdrawn and vanished. One left the gun; the others had left the singers lamenting over their remains. The Office has left its own memorialist, too, he thought as he ran his hand over the blinded side of his face: me.

He got up again and found walking surprisingly easy. I am too young, but that is acceptable. I am scarred, but most of the wounds are on the outside and all but the largest two are healed. Though they are Border Command, they cannot know how to deal with real Special Office people. God, Special Office people barely knew how to deal with themselves.

Better, he murmured, and found the skin loosening around his jaw and cheekbones. "These ironies," he began to the passing warehouses, "are not necessarily self-destructive. They can be as amusing as the tricks of your magicians have been. One can hide inside of them, be protected . . ." He cut himself short when he became aware of how loudly he was speaking; they could be listening, through the walls, from kilometers away.

They might not be the only dangers. There was hunger and thirst. His rations of dried meat would be adequate for another week, and there was water for three or four more days. The wells of the City had always been infused with magic (the properties of those in the red light quarter, he remembered distantly, had been renowned through half the kingdoms of magic). Unnameable plasmas, many which he knew to be imperceptible to his gunsight, could fill the spaces between water molecules. The City could abound in mystical booby traps, snares, hair-triggered spells that might have enough power left to them to kill him.

His steps became more certain. Just like the old days. Perhaps one or two of the men of power remained, disguised as homunculi, or statues, or merged into the very person and being of the unicorn and its attendant.

The war, if one's premises were properly phrased within one's mind, might still be on. The awful gateway of death need not yet be entered to meet the nearest enemy.

The sun was going down and the sky over the walls was illuminated by pink and golden clouds spectacular enough to compare with the fraternal wars of the magicians.

If he had the Office's eye he could carry on the search at night. It was better that he should rest, wait and hope that the ships would be doing the same. He found the town house of a merchant that did not depend on magic to hold its walls together.

He slept on a bed with blue velvet hangings around it, embroidered with the stars the wizards had decreed should hang in the skies of their universe. The room was paneled with oak, carved with bas-reliefs of the commerce of the kingdoms of magic: merchants bartering over spices and rare essences, the trade in slaves (dispirited scientists and soldiers shocked at the irrelevance of their inherent rights and dignity), the dragon-runs where the great beasts were bred and strengthened.

Etridge had personally supervised the placement of the tripods around the ship. There was a moon, so the City was visible in the normal spectrum. The energies that bound it together could be seen through the scopes and sensors, overlaying the walls, rising along with the towers and minarets or running along portions of the avenue that showed through the open Teachers' Door.

"Only the Special Office has seen it like this," Etridge remarked to Stamp as he swung the monocular away from him. "Or like this." The City's jagged outline shone like mercury.

"Until they gave their eyes away." Stamp was intensely depressed.

"I'm sure they kept some for their own. How else could they be able to watch their beloved magicians turn the rest of us into toads?"

"They were not like that."

"No? They were like you, then? Maybe a little more caught up in their own dreams. Enough so they could turn the wizards' crimes into gold and drop their own weapons when they became too powerful and too true for them to handle."

"And *we* are not that way?" Stamp continued, looking at the City and, from the sound of his voice, aging perceptibly.

"Of course not. You've known that for some time," Etridge snorted.

Stamp did not reply, but looked back through the left side windows, up to where the lights of the other ships were bright enough to reveal their colors and keep separate from the stars.

Before he went to sleep, Aden made sure that the room's eastern windows were open and that the bed was positioned in front of them. He was on the fifth floor of a building which was, in turn, set atop a slight rise. The gunsight's infrared range showed that the horizon would be visible over the walls in the morning.

The sun and the morning breeze carried salt air. Gulls circled in front of the windows. Their sharp calls reminded Aden of the morning singing of the City's muezzins when they had come to announce the end of the wizards' testing of each other and that it was safe to honor them again.

Aden awoke quickly. As he had during his first operations for the Office, he waited for his eye to reach through the closed lid and make sure it was safe to move. He had continued doing that after the unicorn had taken the eye, forgotten it and then picked up the habit again in the Taritan Valley, safest and gentlest of all his world's places.

When the engraved eye told him nothing, he opened his own. A thick layer of dust coated the room's furnishings and diffused the sunlight into dream tonalities.

The air muffled the sounds of the City's continuing disintegration and of the gulls singing to the fleets that would follow the ocean to this spot. Aden stretched in the quiet, not wishing to get out from under the blankets.

He swung his feet over the side of the bed, put on his trousers, shirt and boots, and found some dried meat in his pack.

He finished eating and sipped night-cooled wine from his canteen. It comforted him as did the dusty air, and set the various realities that hovered near to him at a bearable distance.

He guessed the hour to be around seven when he reached the street. The sun was coming over the City's walls; it caused the facing buildings and mosaics to flare with stunning radiances. One mosaic, unable to bear the touch of the world's sun, crumbled soundlessly into white dust and drifted down from its supporting wall to the cobblestones.

From Donchak's old store he could orient himself and reach the center of the City. He clipped the holster-stock and the sight onto the pistol. Ranging the nearby streets, he found nothing more than residual energies and lines of force mortaring buildings together or animating decorative statuary.

He could not believe that the City was so deserted. Surely the despair of the magicians could not have infected the common people to the point of suicide too. But a great and fundamental underpinning had been removed from their society. Like the men who had ruled them, they had lived for seven centuries in the demonstrated rightness of a certain universe. Then something had suggested that they were wrong, that the deaths of their sons and fathers had meant nothing, that they had served shadows. The only ones who could have reassured them had discovered the same thing and left. Aden *had* seen the people of the City. They stood dumbly around the imagist in the village park, tried to start farms that would need water and fertilizer, wandering through the mountains seeking gardens where magicians had stopped time.

He walked through the confused streets the wizards had built. At intervals his path was blocked by the rubble of collapsed buildings. His gunsight showed him one heap that was only an illusion of some complexity. This disturbed him for it implied that there might still be some magicians left in the City who could be aware of his presence. Then he examined it more carefully and found that the pile of marble and splintered hardwoods merely represented the decay of an equally imaginary palace.

It had been common to retain a lesser man of power or his assistant to create the illusion of a grander building than that which one really occupied. The practice was much favored by petty merchants and parvenus of all sorts. After all, the City was founded on subjectivity. The power of magic defined reality and such illusions were often appreciated as much as the more respectable mansions built of actual stone and mortar.

Aden stepped into the debris. It offered no resistance, became invisible once he was inside of it and then regained its apparent solidity when he came out on the other side. The comic aspect of the scene was undeniable, and he laughed out loud for the first time since he had left the Taritan.

Etridge, Stamp knew, was tall and sparely built, and would have passed for a banker or a diplomat in any city of his world. He was also strong for his age, and the unhurried arcs of his movements indicated exceptional reserves of energy and strength.

The City was before them, the sun hidden below its walls. The tapering shadows of domes and spiked minarets pointed their darkness at the foothills to the east. The bones and the other hovercraft shone in the new light as it swept down the hillsides toward them. Stamp moved closer to Etridge, holding his automatic rifle in both hands. If one of the magicians or enough of their power remained, and if he found himself still capable of believing in it, he conceived that it would be a sign to overpower or eliminate Etridge. But if the fraud continued to expose itself and if the City kept dissolving before his world's reality, he also knew that he would need Etridge, as desperately as he had once needed his parents and then a woman named Sarah in the places they had each controlled.

Grant and Halstead were standing in front of the hovercraft, waiting for them. Both looked like younger models of Anderton, stocky, well muscled, unexceptional features; perhaps it was a blandness of spirit that permitted them to stand in front of the Holy City with no detectable emotion. Stamp recalled the emotion Anderton had shown before the lights, and thought that it might also be simple courage. They were good, strong men who wished only to end the force that had produced Thorn River as well as the fairy castles; because they followed Etridge did not necessarily mean that they followed his dreams too.

Their uniforms were scrupulously correct. Packets of electronic equipment studded their tunics. Stamp noticed that their weapons gleamed with cold and constant light when the sun reached them. The mosaics and frescoes on the City's walls remained in shadow, and the contrast between the men and the hovercraft, and the City was startling.

Illusion; it means nothing, he thought, and shielded his eyes. I'm starting to think like him.

Etridge carried a small carbine that looked like a hunting piece. Its stock was made from finely grained wood and the engine turnings on the action lent a softness to the metal. It seemed to be intended more as an insult to the City than a threat to whatever might be left inside its walls.

The sentry pylons had been taken down and stowed inside the ship. As always, it suggested the sea with its canted bow and enclosed superstructure. In a few years the ocean would be back and the true ships would be on it, as they should, rather than floating over deserts and the deserted highways of the enemy.

Again: momentum, convergence, inertia building up in amounts sufficient to overwhelm magic's beauty or the sorrow for its passing, and propel them past anything the men of power had dared to dream or question.

"Ready?" Etridge said to the City. He was distinct and sharply defined before Stamp, as if the sound of his voice had closed the final perceptive circuits necessary for the other man to see the world that stood around him with guns and telescopes in its hands.

"We've got as much as we can right now, sir. There's new activity around the central location." Anderton was commanding the ship. No one questioned the wisdom of Etridge walking outside.

"How so?" Communication would be by voice with the ship following them, watching over their progress.

"Customary variations on existing wavelengths and resonances."

"Anything unusual in that?"

"Only in concentration and variety. It doesn't look like anything we couldn't untangle if we waited."

Etridge considered this for a moment. "No reason to wait. Gentlemen." He glanced at Stamp on his right and at Grant and Halstead back alongside the ship, and stepped forward.

The air was quite still. In between the sounds of the decaying city were those of the men walking, quickly joined by the whistling of the hovership's engines. Stamp looked back and saw the dust clouding out from the inflating plenum skirt. The ship rocked a little and then rose a meter from the road.

Up in the foothills, the sun reflected off the armored surfaces of the other ship. Stamp felt more relaxed than he had thought he would be, neither did he feel desolate as he had before.

Etridge set an easy pace so it took a few minutes to reach the Teachers' Door. It was built from slabs of pale granite that had been fused into a single archway, seventy meters square. Strangely wrought projections of black iron and bronze were spotted along its inner surfaces; they were the physical points on which many of the Gate's non-corporeal doors were attached. Behind them the two main doors had been left open.

In contrast to the frescoed and mosaiced walls around them, the doors were blank metal, charred like wood along their edges. Anderton informed them over the loudspeaker that the other doors of magic had provided the color and ornamentation the wizards so loved.

Stamp gripped his rifle more tightly to stabilize himself against the sight of the interior City. Its exterior had been unitary, complete, bound together by its muraled walls against their approach. Inside, it fragmented into innumerable parts, as if it were a diadem suddenly hurled against a wall in a fit of anger.

They entered upon an avenue leading directly east, so that it appeared to end in the new sun. On either side its light gilded the rotting buildings. Statues and allegorical figures with the limbs and faces of beasts moved in abbreviated, repetitive gestures.

"See it?" Etridge confided from the side of his mouth. "Just as it was outside the walls with the bone heaps and the singers. Everything devoted to show and ornament." He waved condescendingly at the ruined statues, and several of them obligingly cracked and fell apart as they passed. Etridge had known that they would before they had gone in, but the effect was worthwhile. Grant and Halstead joked to each other and Stamp found himself fighting back a tentative smile.

"The Avenue of Wisdom," Anderton informed them.

"The appropriateness of our path continues, don't you think?" Etridge, again looking straight ahead and speaking conversationally.

Stamp had memorized the aerial views of the City, so he knew the name of the street as it was spoken in the magicians' speech. He also knew, as did Etridge, that many of the triumphal columns and gesturing figures that lined the street commemorated the victories of magic: Heartbreak Ridge, the Third Perimeter, Kells.

If Etridge was as human as he pretended to be, his calculated arrogance might be as much defensiveness as from any intoxication with anticipated discoveries in the ash heaps. Stamp looked about him as he walked, and decided that if it was true, Etridge's capacity for absolutes would render such a distinction meaningless. Etridge could carry the guilt of a hundred Thorn Rivers inside of himself and still chase his enemies, or their ghosts, or their founding gods until they all dropped from exhaustion.

A dying cyclops limped toward them from a side street. Its single eye was blank and yellowed, and its skin was gray with the mortal rot of Etridge's world. Stamp guessed that it lived because it was too stupid to understand itself. Etridge could understand it and he signaled Grant and Halstead to hold their fire while the ship examined the creature.

It continued to move toward them, obscene, shredded genitals hanging between its legs, the remains of quilted silk and gold mesh armor on its shoulders. Three years ago it had been happily passing its eternal life crushing the enemies of its master; three nights ago, Stamp would have cried to see its ruin so clearly.

Etridge kept walking at his deliberate pace. The sun lit up his face and uncovered a symmetry identical to the hovership's, calm and immovable and ultimately unaware of the strength the cyclops might retain because they were looking through him, using what magic remained to him as a lens that focused the antennas and reflector dishes on the more distant secrets of its dead master.

Anderton said something and Etridge raised his gun. The small weapon hardly bucked and for a second the monster stopped and stood, glaring ridiculously at them. His skin then lightened and granulated like sand drying after a wave. When he was almost white his eye dusted away, the particles falling straight down in the windless air, and then his head, and then the torso, all falling down upon themselves.

Etridge made a point of walking through the powder that was left. Stamp wondered if they might not be going too far out of their way to trample on graves. But that, he remembered from the notebooks, was the idea.

The ship passed over the dust too, and when it was gone the paving stones were clean.

Aden was gratified to find the house so easily. He had taken only two wrong turns before coming upon it. The flags and carpets were gone, so he did not immediately recognize it. But the blue tiled street was the same, as were the perilously overhanging houses and the smell, though all of this was now thickly overlain with rain-clotted dust.

Except for the desertion and neglect, the quarter had survived the wizards' retreat much better than he had first thought. From the hills, the scope had shown him disintegrating roofs and walls, their edges chipped and charred as if a burning rake had been drawn over them. But the walls here were put together with solid stone and cement and faced with marble slabs hung on iron pegs. The statues in front of the more prosperous establishments were respectfully immobile, though they did copy the style and pose of those in front of the magicians' palaces. If the materials were merely physical, their design, the twisting streets and high towers reflected the tastes of magic.

Some of the businessmen of the City had perceived that they could not take it with them, or did not care to go to the places where you could, and so felt no need for memorialists or animated gryphons fanning their grave sites with stone wings, reciting their genealogies until time ended.

Aden struck his hand against his head to drive these thoughts away. The wires were on fire again, the voice of the dead Office leading him on to claim what they had specifically denied him.

The houses leaned over the street. This might have been what Donchak was feeling, he told himself, because this might have been what he was trying to do.

The eye, he repeated to himself, the eye. I must move toward it. If I do not then it may be shown that I am only responding to pressures and stresses imposed by magic, my world, and the Office standing between the two, and that I have no will of my own.

He entered Donchak's house, brushing aside cobwebs and decayed rugs. No power remained in the latter, or at least none that the gunsight could show him. As it had in the merchant's house the dust in the air masked everything in afternoon light, slowing it as if the place had already been removed from present reality and into memory. He asked himself why nothing in his own world had ever seemed so tender and remote. Gedwyn's face rose before him from underneath the Office's healing scars. The sound of his own sharpened breath drove it away.

Aden focused his eye; it seemed more acute in this half-light. He had been in the building one evening, years ago, but still remembered the placement of the furniture, now overturned, the arrangement of the rooms and where Donchak's elaborate tea service had been.

He went over to the serving table, opened the teapot and saw a crust of dried sugar on its bottom. He smelled it and caught a lingering hint of a drug that had been fashionable in polite society when he was last there.

He put down the service and walked into the back room. His orientation, though it was now in daylight instead of by the moon, brought him to the garden in the rear of the building. There were burn stains on the flagstones where the trivial magics Donchak's customers once paid him with had turned from luminous flowers back into the sulfurous compounds from which they had been made.

The wrought iron gate had been blasted off its hinges and lay half-embedded in the stucco wall across the alley.

Aside from the dust, Aden noticed that the ruin was clean. Though deprived of souls, the artificial beings and homunculi the magicians had left behind had still hungered. Apparently, they had fed on the City's garbage while they waited for their masters to order them to war upon themselves. The favorites of the kingdoms fed on year-old fish guts and offal while his world ate sparingly of meat and knowledge, waiting in its air-conditioned bunkers for the screaming and chanting from the east to end.

He stayed in the neighborhoods of the common folk for more time than he should have. The streets continued their turnings with more sensuosity than he recalled, but the course of his progress traced his memory with surprising accuracy. The nondescript contours of the merchants' quarters had impressed themselves as deeply upon one section of his intelligence as the majesty of the City's greater works had on another.

When he reached the square, he found its dimensions as for-

eign as those of Donchak's building had been reassuringly familiar. The gun came to his shoulder and showed him lemon and
saffron plasmas pouring from the fountain. They curled and
spurted from the splintered necks and craniums of mermaids;
contradictory shadows played over the statuary and the paving
blocks around the fountain, blanketing the midmorning light
through all the dimensions perceptible to the gun.

The plasmas rose more than a hundred meters and then fell in
asymmetrical arcs to the fountain and the square. From there
they ran in broad streams that reached to the surrounding buildings before they disappeared into the paving stones or evaporated
into a whiskey-colored mist. Through it, twisted homunculi
limped, blowing on bone flutes or on bagpipes with bellows made
from the scrotal sacs of gryphons.

Aden gasped and ducked back into the alley, as Donchak had
made him do ages ago. The memorialists walked past him. None
that he had seen on his way into the City had done more than
play their instruments or sing; they had never moved from the
site they were meant to commemorate. That was their function;
that was why they had been created.

Aden felt his heart quicken. Sweat accumulated on his skull
and seemed to increase the conductance of his cranial net; it was
singing with a volume that threatened to drown out the
memorialists. If only he could find some kind of sense in the electric humming, something beyond mere suspicion or feeling to tell
him what the Office wanted. If only, for once in its vague centuries, the Office would say something clearly, specifically,
definitely, even if it was nothing more than, yes, we still live and
exist, and, therefore, so do you. That would be enough. Enough
to assure him that the song was not the sympathetic resonances
that the hovercrafts' searching radiations struck in the wires.

As he watched, two memorialists came through the opened
doors of the cathedral. They were transfixed in the sight's cross
hairs, framed by the melted forms of mermen and shrouded by
the billowing plasmas. The two circled around the square and
passed in front of where he hid; then out of the plaza to an avenue which he remembered to have been named after a woman.

More artificial beings appeared in groups that became loose formations, all dragging themselves out of the cathedral's darkness, down its monumental stairs and across the plaza, each one stumbling along to his own discordant tune, each new group prodding a surprised burst of electric thought from the Office's gun. He felt its weight and texture changing against his cheek as it modified the composition of its ammunition to deal with each successive creature, and then modified its own structure to deal with the recoil and firing of its transmuted bullets.

The gun was a thing of infinite consideration and accommodation, continually adjusting itself to suit both the worlds of science and magic. If the creatures of magic were to be slain, it would be with bullets that were, ultimately, made of magic, rather than its tangible duplication. If the target was from Aden's world, as the tanks had been, the instrument would operate along lines of rigidly defined masses and energies. What, he wondered briefly, painfully, had the gun formulated for Gedwyn?

In its every aspect, the gun was an extension of the Office. Aden wished that its strength would fill the gaps so many years of equivocation and balancing between the absolutes had left in him. There should have been a normal history inside of him where conviction and doubt alternated, as did the feelings of love and hatred, loyalty and deceit, defining a median between the opposing extremes. Instead there was only the attempt at the median itself without supportive feelings on either side.

The magical creatures increased in number and variety. Tall humanoids draped in dignified togas of jet silk marched down the wide steps to the square. In contrast to the memorialists, they neither played nor sang but maintained silence in the one auditory spectrum open to Aden. They carried long tapers that were unlit in the spectrum of visible light, but which his gunsight showed to be blindingly aflame in three others; the fires, gold, turquoise and amethyst, swirled upward around their heads, illuminating their austere and unnaturally drawn features with a startling radiance.

Tame cerberuses paced quietly at their heels. They wore

chains of linked and beaded diamonds around each of their three necks.

Other creatures in the shapes of men followed the taper bearers. The gunsight showed them to be made and motivated by simple enchantments; even Aden had some rough idea of the physics upon which the magicians had unconsciously based their lives. They were cast from metal, and the chromium brightness of their skin reflected the noon sun as brilliantly as dragon's hide; the lines of their idealized faces suggested the wounded severity that Aden had observed in some Border fortress commanders.

They were dressed in dark blue velvet knickers and tunics with white hose, trimmed in a lace that was yellow and then ruby in successive spectrums. Each one carried a black cushion upon which rested some crown or decoration or medal.

The gunsight brought the decorations close enough for Aden to marvel at their intricate beauty. Although static and limited, the coronets and medals not only occupied distinct presences along each of the spectrums open to him, but also clearly implied honors that could be understood only through a grasp of all the worlds in which the men of power had held sway.

Understood.

These too, were memorialists. They were deafeningly silent, but they expressed the memory of someone powerful beyond imagining, who had won these tokens of honor and courage in adventures near the the borderlines of death and unreality.

So great a man as that, the gun reminded him, was gone. Not killed, or driven into exile, but fled before something more terrible than himself or any power he might dare summon to stand with him against it.

Aden wondered if he could hear the wailing of the hovership over the silence of the creatures. Not yet.

Diamonds, rubies, opals and sapphires that held all the darkness of the ocean the wizards had sent away, glimmered on the chains of knightly orders, locked and suspended in filigrees of platinum and iridium, stitched as the memorialists had been in the cross hairs. Their mystery and symbolism should have been unapproachable. Aden whispered: yet I have defined them, calculated their range, atomic weights, compositions, meanings, constructed projectiles to shatter them, and all with a machine that is at least half magical itself and therefore incapable of such complete understanding.

Grave and imperial, twelve ranks of the silver-skinned men walked down the steps of the cathedral. Straggling memorialists scampered around them, baiting the cerberuses, blowing on flutes and pipes, their grating songs emphasizing their silence. It reminded Aden of nothing so much as a funeral.

When the great men of his own world died, either naturally, or by the assaults of magic turning them to stone in their studies or into salt on a battlefield, much was done to mark their passing. Perhaps it had only seemed like a great deal in contrast to the cold, unrelenting rationality his world had adopted in all its other dealings with life and the enemy.

First, there had always been the regiments of foot and horse and their bands playing the slow songs of morning. The pipers from the highland units were always the most poignant to Aden. They marched with a briefly halting step that seemed to dam up the skirl of their instruments until what reached the listener was an essence of wild sadness.

After that would be chamberlains and other functionaries, displaying the honors of the deceased on velvet pillows. On the dead men's orders and medals, Aden suddenly remembered, there had been dragons and centaurs and all the other mythic creatures that had been driven from his world when they assumed actual, physical reality. But, at these times, they still attended the great, dead men of his world in miniature, surrounded by jewels and mottoes in archaic languages, wrapped about with the music of regimental pipes.

If one continues the parallel, he thought, and if it truly is that creatures of magic serve the men of power in life, but in death shift their allegiance to those of my own world . . . where has their treason occurred, and why? Magic had always been thought of as having been reborn; Gedwyn had told him that. What had drawn the unicorns away from it the first time and convinced them that they should live their fragile, eternal lives on the medals, commemorating the achievements of his own world?

I am personifying again, he muttered through closed jaws. But (always *but*, never *if*, as it had been before the Wizards' War) that was the first hinge of the conflict, that the allegories and metaphors and stories had regained literal truth and power.

But (again), we never lost it. His hand held the gun more tightly. His index finger was pressed painfully against the outside of the trigger guard.

The unicorn emerged onto the cathedral's portico surrounded by solemn black archers and falconers with eagles on their cocked arms. Its attendant, his gleaming body still swarming with the tumult of battle and the hunt, walked blindly at its side. When Aden had first seen him, he had been kneeling toward the altar, looking away from him. Now he could see that he had no face, just an elliptical surface that was reminiscent of the doctor's at the hospital, except that hundreds of tiny cavalrymen charged and retreated across it, then gave way to the coronation pageants of princes that had died long ago. He had no genitals, no fingernails, pores, openings, nothing to imply the flawed and fragmentary life that animated the memorialists.

Aden took out the hilt-piece he had picked up near the first bone pile to find a face for the being. The dryad's eyes opened and stared awkwardly to the side until Aden turned it toward the parade. Tear tracks became visible on the carved wooden face, although it did not change expression.

Aden watched and felt its density increase until the fragment was like a lead sinker in his hand and its eyes lost all power of movement or suggestion of life. These acts, he thought, must have drained its last quanta of power. Now it is like the stones of the City and will, in time, transmute into dust.

Last night this would have terrified him or increased the bleakness of his heart. Today, he found that it fit into the center of this City and into the observation of this parade. If the gunsight had been versatile enough he might have been able to perceive the path along which its power fled, discover whether it dissipated into the air or if it was recalled by one of the chamberlains across the square who had decided that the dryad's face would be better suited to the neck chain of the decoration he carried, rather than in the hand of Aden.

The face would not have fit the attendant anyway. Aden put the piece of wood back into his breast pocket and returned his left hand to the bottom of the pistol's magazine.

The crowd of chamberlains, memorialists, lancers mounted on gryphons, archers, taper bearers and falconers made it difficult to keep the unicorn in sight. Still, it was as tall as he remembered it to have been; the arch of its gleaming neck rose above its escort, and the point of its horn was at least four meters from the ground.

They crossed the portico and descended the stairs. From there they moved slowly to their left, following the perimeter of the square and then crossing between him and the fountain. Aden caught the unicorn in the gunsight and tried to determine whether the eye was still there. He found that the creature did not even exist in the fourth spectrum; but that was a place of limited phenomena, and the unicorn's creator apparently had not thought it worthwhile to occupy. The eye, however, did. It floated alone in the air, serene and independent, protectively encircled by lavender wraiths and gryphons.

The wires blazed under his scalp at levels approaching actual pain. The gun hummed so loudly as it digested the incoming radiations from the parade that Aden was afraid one of the passing creatures might hear it.

He dialed the sight to probe the last three spectrums. The unicorn was present in each of these, the beauty of its movements unaffected by the alien lights and presences that surrounded it. In the sixth, the eye was silver and nearly indistinguishable from the ornamentation of the unicorn's chanfron. In the seventh, it was like a faceted diamond, patterned by its interior circuitries, while in the eighth it lost its corporeal substance and evidenced its singularity only by a blue aureole of long-wave radiation.

A sound drifted up one of the angled streets that opened onto the square. Aden noted it, but it had to grow from vague indirection to a distinct purring before his conscious mind detached itself from the sight of the unicorn. When it did, he felt his heart and mind suddenly slam against each other and flatten into two dimensions.

He turned back to the parade. Nothing showed that any of them had seen or heard. The main group—where was the catafalque? there should be a gun carriage if this was to be a proper funeral, an ancient caisson with the flag-draped coffin on it—continued at its measured pace. The unicorn itself was within two hundred meters of where he was hiding.

The eye jerked around as he watched, sweeping past him and then aiming at the far end of the square where the first taper bearers were.

"It knows," Aden whispered to the gun and to whoever might be listening to the wires in his skull. "Of course it knows," he went on for himself and for the benefit of the listeners. "How could the eye be there for years and not have it learn how to see with it." Aden's voice rose involuntarily.

A memorialist shaped like a hairless baboon raised his head from his flute and looked directly at Aden. It was thirty meters away, but the gunsight brought it close enough to let its dead, enchanted eyes bracket the vertical line of the cross hairs.

The gun examined the creature, selected its ammunition and fired with a sound no louder than the air at evening. It guarded its muzzle flash as it appeared in all of the spectrums open to it. When the player dropped only the unicorn noticed.

Another memorialist, this one a dwarf in a harlequin's costume, dragged the carcass away from the line of march, obviously concerned that it might cause one of the taper bearers or chamberlains to miss a step. As he took it away, the corpse first turned olive, then tan, and then scattered away as if it were made from leaves.

Aden knew that his finger had stayed on the outside of the trigger guard. This did not trouble him any more than it had when the gun had fired on the tank column.

The unicorn, or at least its eye had seen. It turned its face toward him and Aden found it too beautiful to carry only terror with it. The eye, being a thing of rationality, should have been beyond the reach of anything made so purely of magic. But the creature had found a philosophic bridge, and had possibly translated the information the eye collected from the world around it into terms comprehensible to it. If the eye and the unicorn had become a single thing, they would be as removed from the two enemy worlds as Aden felt himself to be, as the Special Office truly was.

It *is* different, he became convinced. The gun butt was slick and warm in his hand. Its power made it special even before Donchak had taken it and given it to the unicorn. Now it and the unicorn had both become something different. He wavered in his desire and awe of the eye alone.

He felt something like hope for a moment. A synthesis of some kind had been achieved and a middle ground discovered which might be occupied by magic and rationality at the same time. This could be the peace that had eluded the world for seven hundred years.

Weakness came into his joints, and his chest was filled with the wet cotton feeling of fear. Simply because so wondrous a being as the unicorn had combined the antagonistic realities within itself did not mean that its achievement could be shared. And even if it could, if individual human spirits could be made great and strong enough to reconcile the torrents of contradiction that the unicorn's own eye and the Office's must have been reporting, there was no longer anything left to compel his world to accept it. *They* had triumphed. The unicorn's achievement was a bitter joke upon them all.

They are coming in this triumph of theirs, he murmured to the unicorn. They are the hunters again. The duality of your vision cannot protect you any more than it protected Donchak or the Office.

The eye was still centered in the gunsight. The unicorn may have nodded its head in response, or the movement may have been a reflexive jerk caused by the sound of the approaching turbines.

Up and down the parade, various beings slowed and stopped. They turned their heads questioningly, each looking through the one or several spectrums which their creators had allowed to them. Each found a different thing, and so they reacted in different ways, some with what Aden took to be fear, others with indifference, others with eager curiosity. It was difficult to read their expressions.

Whatever emotions the unicorn's face might have revealed were hidden by its chanfron. Only the two eyes showed. The black and golden horn moved like a metronome against the fountain's plasmas.

Again: the caisson? Who among all the millions of things and beings that have died here is all, any of this meant to commemorate?

Aden ducked out of the doorway and darted across the street to the building opposite him. It was made from granite blocks and its stolidity marked it as a former government office. No attempt had been made to decorate it or to disguise its origins despite its prominent location. This meant that Aden would be obvious to anyone that happened to look in that direction. Without any masking powers or presences even the gun would appear as a fire.

That did not matter. The unicorn had already seen him, and it was inconceivable that the ship had not had him under some kind of surveillance since morning. In either event, he was small and of little consequence.

He crept along a columned arcade until he was almost out into the square. From where he stopped, the cathedral was partially blocked by the fountain, but he had a clearer view of thè far end of the area.

The ship only seemed to be near to him because of its size and the arrogant clarity of its lines. Four men were walking in front of it. One was dressed in black while the rest were in a gray that matched the building stones around him.

The gun reported them to be human. They existed in the same form and in the same limited way in each of the parallel spectrums. The guns they carried with them were equally simple and unitary, as was the absoluteness of their function.

Conversely, the hovercraft following them was a thing of vast complexity. The sight showed it alternately sucking every scrap of information from the dimensions around it, and then unleashing great torrents of active-probing radiations. In two of the spectrums the hovercraft's antennas aimed such amounts of inquisitory energy at the parade that inexplicable shadows were cast behind the fountain, outlining not only its statuary but also the plasma jets, as if the ship was the sun and the magic of the fountain was a darkness in the world.

Dish and flat panel antennas rotated slowly, carefully on top of the hovercraft. Their pace matched the maddeningly relaxed step of the four men in front of it.

Was this to be the caisson and catafalque? Aden suddenly asked the gun. Could it be that the unicorn had summoned *them*, as it had the sorcerous throng and possibly Aden himself? So many meanings: as if he were in a room roofed and walled with mirrors and prisms, each reflecting a different image and then breaking and commingling light from others, reflecting back on each other, drawing more and more tightly together in an antagonistic circularity that enveloped him completely.

The line of marchers spread out laterally as they hit some invisible barrier twenty meters from the ship.

Though they were turning on curving, bending paths, the beings continued to move forward. Aden saw them stiffen, rise on their twisted spines, drop their instruments and then turn away from the whirling antennas. He adjusted the controls on the scope, as much to find reassurance in their solidity as to sweep the open spectrums. The stone column stayed cool and linear alongside his body.

Despite the alienness of the memorialists' faces, or those of the taper bearers, he thought he could find a common line of knowledge, despair and demoralization. Whether their eyes were made from stones set in ape's skulls, or of sapphires in the faces of godly abstraction, he discovered the same slackening, the same absent redirection downward to the paving stones, the same tentative gestures of their hands or claws toward their heads as if to catch the furious storm of knowledge the antennas were forcing upon them.

THE SIEGE OF WONDER

The second man from the left nervously ran his hand along the action of his rifle and compressed his eyebrows in fear and mystification at what was happening before him. But that was all. The other three were impassive.

The ship played its high siren wail behind them, rocking on its air bubble. Its guns and rocket launchers stayed fixed and all the motion of its antennas was circular; like the magicians, its greatest power lay in simple gestures made to the accompaniment of certain words, under auspicious alignments of certain stars. The ship had no need for inelegant displays of destructive power.

The men stepped forward. The members of the funeral parade stood in front of them for a second. Then they turned away, facing fully toward Aden again. They had been buried in enough information to suspect from what and how they had been made.

They found, suspended in the simple web of Aden's gunsight, that their heritage and ancestry were in free helium, dust, deuterium, splintered wood and the leavings of dogs.

Others had found that they were nothing more than thoughts, the compacted wave fronts of wizardly imaginations. When they saw this, their own sustaining beliefs in themselves faltered and then crumbled. They dissolved from physical actuality back into the nothing from which they had been formed.

No wonder the servants of magic were often so grand, Aden concluded, when many of them were imaginations made actual. Created thusly, they had never been compelled to make any concessions to either of the real worlds.

Aden examined their faces as they blew away and, unlike the others which were bound, however distantly, to the substance of the world, detected resignation and even contentment.

The rest acknowledged the horror and watched their magnificent clothes, finely wrought weapons and their own limbs rotting through a progression of more stable compounds. They saw this and knew, irrevocably, why it was happening and why nothing else could happen.

All the dreams of glory that they had saved from the departure of the magicians crossed their faces and ended as they walked away from the ship on disintegrating feet, and then on their hands and the stumps of legs turning to sand and sawdust.

Wailing, more terrible than what he remembered from the convoys of refugees fleeing Thorn River, reached him over the ship's engines. He was witnessing a battle being fought completely on the terms of his own world for there were no more men of power left to shape new energies to confound the inductive apparatus of the ship.

The unicorn with its attendant had stopped. Drawn like sleepwalkers, their guard of gryphon-cavalry and archers left them and proceeded cautiously toward the ship. They looked stronger than the taper bearers or chamberlains. Muscles built from essential energy pulsed under the gryphons' golden fur; the riders were armored like knights, protected by terrible charms and talismans.

Their strength would mean nothing. The ship was luring them with its open challenge to their power and to their belief that their own reality was ultimately sacred and therefore beyond knowing.

He considered shooting them. If they died, it would be as whole, functioning beings; their lives' mystery would be translated into the greater mystery of death. They were only the created, not the creators, and so would not know of the possibility of this escape. But they were not the ones he should risk revealing himself for.

The gryphons and their riders ended in the same way the memorialists had. Some vanished so quickly and completely that Aden had trouble being sure if they had existed at all; since they were only thoughts to begin with, their end erased their memory as well as their present physical reality. He recalled them, seconds after they were gone, only in impossibly distant suspicions and flashes of déjà vu.

The rest went more slowly. They reached the twenty-meter line around the ship, stood there a moment, and then faced around to Aden, walking, it appeared, into the earth as their bodies crumbled. The ship had shown them the dark that had always been under their feet. They had been created as lights and beacons against it, but the gulf had been larger than the magicians had suspected.

This kept on for half an hour. Then all of them were gone. Aden estimated that there had been three to four thousand individuals, every one of them fashioned from some kind of magic. Within an hour all their lives had been transformed into formulae, Llwyellan Functions, micro-dots and Henschel profiles.

The four men began walking toward the unicorn, and the ship followed them like an immense pet. Its air cushion kicked up thick clouds of the funeral dust into the air, where a new breeze caught it. The gunsight showed the cloud to be comprised only of static elements, devoid of energy or animation.

The dust fell on his clothes and the gun's barrel. Aden worried for a moment that it might clog the weapon's delicate mechanisms, then decided that it was too late for such thoughts. He leaned out from behind the column. The unicorn and its attendant were where they had stopped when the hovership first came into the square. The dust of their thousands of retainers and protectors also settled on the unicorn's flanks and on the attendant's shoulders, dulling the brilliance of its coverings and tumult of his skin.

The City was empty with shocking finality. Even that morning, there had been the promising threat of lingering magic strong enough to survive the ship. Now the City was a complete ruin, occupied only by its conquerors and its last refugees.

Stamp watched them becoming shrouded in the fog of their own dissolution. They spread out as they came toward the ship, tripping over the ones that had fallen in front of them. He saw them piling up in a wide sweep before him, their colors and hideous forms blurring together, sinking into the paving stones as they milled forward and then away.

Anderton spoke to them from inside the ship. The parade's wailings did not drown him out for he was talking in frequencies the dying could not scream in; the ship adjusted that for him.

The effect was comforting, for it lent a feeling of detachment from the horror meters in front of him. It was as if they were only watching a film or hologram of something that had happened long ago.

There had been no sorrow in anything he had seen since they left the forest. Small fractions of pity and curiosity, but little else. The city had proven itself to be as fragile as Etridge accused it of being. The self-destruction of the magicians' servants outside the walls had repelled him. It was a stupid exercise in self-indulgence.

All he had wanted was a gesture worthy of their own myth. Instead he faced the dried-out husks of puppets, phony, impotent monuments to millennial frauds. Everything faded before Etridge and the coldness of his ship.

As they had walked down the Avenue of Wisdom, the ship's radars had discovered an actual magician, locked and embalmed inside an egg of frozen time, in a garden near the square. In a fit of unbidden helpfulness, the computers had come up with the formula explaining how it had been done five seconds after they had charted its location. Two minutes later they produced a formula to crack the spell. Etridge did not think it worth the trouble for the printouts also showed that the magician had died as a consequence of its casting.

Anderton's voice continued, needlessly explaining the mechanics of the ruin occurring in front of them. He noted that the number of creatures was rapidly diminishing, but that the unicorn had not joined in their march; it remained behind, five hundred thirty-two meters from the prow of the ship. Its attendant was with it. It had the eye.

Anderton also noted that the presence they had detected that morning was with them again, hiding in an arcade directly west of where the unicorn was standing. He was human and had been with the Special Office before its official closing. Would Etridge require more?

"No." The parade had destroyed itself. A last memorialist ran back and forth through the dust of his companions, gibbering repulsively. He tripped and fell, exploding into white ash like a dandelion blossom. Etridge raised a set of field glasses, surveyed the square and then motioned them ahead.

Stamp found himself walking easily, taking long, relaxed strides. He could make out the contours of the unicorn and its attendant. Their scale was diminished by the emptiness of the square, and the spaces around them were vacant of any enchantment. There were no memorialists left, no bearers of candles or honors, nothing to block the intrusion of his own world into those spaces, to stop it from extending outward around the isolated unicorn, over the City, over the half of the planet occupied by the men of power, outward too, into the sky and the regions closed to god.

Anderton's voice acquired a relaxed assurance as they crossed the paving stones. The air bubble of the ship kept blowing the creatures' piled dust into the air, lifting it and sending it over them as they walked. At times the dust shoaled thickly, becoming a tan mist that permitted him to stare directly into the sun; it hid the walled horizon and the buildings enclosing the square, suspending the unicorn and its companion like raindrops in a blank sky.

Stamp could not believe that this was what Etridge and the other Border commanders had wanted. All Anderton and Bock wanted was an end. But the commanders must have spent their waking nights expanding strategic maps into tactical diagrams, smothered with continually increasing numbers of arrows: green, brown, silver, black arrows thrusting against the shadow-enemy, enfilading his flanks, blocking his routes of escape, herding him and his enchantments into indestructible, sterile bell jars. And then, more explicitly, the reality of where the arrow points and the shadows interfaced, smeared with fire and lights rocketing back and forth against the parallel spectrums.

This, he thought as he walked through the coarse haze, should have been the time when the ramjet bombers would have finally sought out the aristocratic men, dressed in their splendid robes, attended by legions of fabulous beasts.

He glanced at Etridge, but found that he could not tell if the man had ever conceived of the ending in such a way. Whatever sort of idea Etridge may have saved for this time, it would have been molded by the thought of Thorn River and what he had done there; it could not have helped but act like a lens upon the man's perceptions and dreams. Like the eye of the Special Office, or that of the unicorn, or Joust Mountain itself.

The wind dispersed the dust and the air was clear again. Stamp cradled his rifle in the crook of his left arm and brushed some of it from his sleeves. He did not realize the arrogance of the gesture until he watched Etridge do the same.

Etridge came closer and handed him his binoculars; they had a small gyrostabilizer in them, so they were no problem to use while walking. The man-being did not surprise Stamp. He had seen any number of animated statues and artificial humans as they had traveled through the City, and one more, no matter how wondrously constructed or covered with miniature universes, could do much more to his senses.

The unicorn, however, touched him across the distance that remained. Like the attendant, it was covered by what might have as easily been its skin as armor, all of it etched with designs of elusive complexity. Its right eye glowed and flickered in its socket, flame like, having no iris or pupil to indicate the direction of its stare. There was a burning in its left eye socket too, but it was dimmer, behind, or possibly inside the jeweled human-ness of the Special Office's eye; that one was clearly fixed on them.

Stamp unconsciously slowed, becoming absorbed in the perfection of the unicorn's features and proportions. It was, he conceived with the exaggerated distance of memory, everything he had once thought the kingdoms of magic to be: outwardly magnificent, with an interior reality so foreign to the thinking of his world as to be beyond its mortalities and brutal, knife-edged hungerings.

The eye fit into its lines and presences. In theory, that should have been impossible. The eye should have qualified and flawed the unicorn; instead it strengthened the creature with its knowledge, turning it into something that did not need the magicians.

"We're under attack from them," Anderton reported over the

ship's speaker. His voice again sounded harsh and strident without the screaming of the dying underneath it.

Etridge held out his free hand with the palm toward the ground. The three other men and the hovercraft obediently stopped. Stamp heard nothing beyond Anderton and the ship's drag skids.

"Any problems?" Etridge asked conversationally. He motioned again, and Stamp returned the binoculars.

"A bit more than we'd anticipated, sir. Could you come closer to the ship? It'd be easier to protect you here." Grant and Halstead backed up with their rifles raised across their chests. Etridge walked casually back, half turning away from the unicorn.

Stamp reached the ship and pressed his back against the flexible plenum skirt. Air escaping from it felt cool against his ankles. They had been on their feet since they entered the City at the Teachers' Door.

The coolness emphasized the noontime heat in the square. Though it was late summer, the temperature was rising above any possibly normal level. Stamp felt sweat collecting under his arms and dripping down along his ribs. He looked at his watch: 1:00. They had been in the square one hour and five minutes.

The fear building inside of him hinted that this was neither a season of their own world or of magic's, but something new which Etridge might not understand and which, in its understanding of him, could escape, hiding and stalking them through interwoven thickets of magic and rationality.

Stamp knew his mouth and throat were dry. It was inconceivable that the eye would not have been discovered by the men of power without the unicorn participating in the deception.

The centuries of the war had been defined sharply. Betrayal and treason were nothing more than the maintaining of an allegiance for one side while serving the other. Then there was the Special Office, becoming lost to the services and then to itself; now the unicorn. They were *apart* from either world, he thought in his fear; a universe of ungovernable multiplicities suddenly rose before him.

"Signals into the area showing up too." Anderton's voice was disjointed and implied a great deal of preoccupation with the defense against the unicorn.

"From where?" The heat made Etridge's words sound more emotional than they really were.

The pauses between Anderton's replies became longer. "Outside. From home, somewhere. It's very weak and we're only getting it through augmentation with the other unit." A full minute of silence from the ship. "The broadcast . . . This is remarkable! I'd never thought that thing capable of so much new stuff!"

"The broadcast?" Stamp found himself saying ingenuously.

"No, goddammit! The goddamn horse out there!" The loudspeaker roughened Anderton's irritation and turned the rebuke into defensive anger.

Quiet.

"Are we losing?" Etridge inquired mildly. He was looking toward the unicorn and so addressed it, rather than the ship.

"Ah . . ." Voices were undercutting Anderton's. "No. No, I don't think so."

"What about the signal, then?"

"It's to a receiver in this area, using a cross-spectrum wave front. Looks like a variation on what the people at Lake . . ." More delay, more voices from the men away from the speaker mike; ". . . from Lake Gilbert."

"Special Office character?" Etridge's words were melting with the heat and his outward calm could not protect them.

"Yes. Or at least like it. Our man is in the area of reception."

Etridge's face closed its protective planes, muscles bunched under his dry skin and scar lines that had been invisible flamed into redness, spelling out the memory of Thorn River and all the suppressed agonies that revolved around it. He feels the world breaking apart too, Stamp thought; something is thrusting upward, underneath us. "All right. I want it, and the thing beside it if you can get him. Shoot to block its path of travel until we can get some kind of control on it."

Etridge walked through the furnace air. Stamp's palms were still slippery, and he had trouble grasping his rifle when he followed. He raised it tentatively. The unicorn and its rider swam in the space above the iron sights, more insubstantial and equivocal than they had been in the dust.

Streams of perspiration coursed down Etridge's face too. His paleness gleamed like the ship's. But his eyes were almost glowing like the unicorn's right eye: no pupils or irises, just mad illumination and fanatic purpose drilled into sheets of white metal.

Stamp forced his breathing into regular patterns. The effort required him to restrain his fear and to keep walking carefully, one booted foot in front of the other with the same cadence as the ship's antennas.

"Come on. Come on." Etridge, strained and urgent. He was gesturing outward with both hands, the little rifle in his right, motioning Stamp and the other two men to spread out. "Block its exits. Don't let it out of the square."

". . . the square?" Stamp muttered to himself. "The thing's nearly stopped the ship and he wants us to corral it?" He found this ludicrous, and it gave him a moment of clarity. The City is deserted, yet I feel it to be overrun by unknown presences, secret agencies, madmen, lunatics, spies. He wondered if this was how they had felt on the first day of the Wizards' War.

Aden could not tell whether it was the heat alone, or if the wires were at last making sense. The net pounded against his mind with a symmetry it had not had before, and which he distantly connected with the days when there was an annunciator connected to it; that had allowed the Office to speak directly into his brain with the tone and inflection of his own thoughts.

He looked at the unicorn through the gunsight and saw great, violent sheets of metallic light unfolding from its guarded head and horn, blanketing the spaces perceptible to him and reaching out to smother the ship and the walking men.

There were shields around them that dulled the light and turned it aside. Their composition must have been infinitely complex, shifting without reference to linear time to meet the battering of the unicorn's magic. More than the unicorn, the shields were largely beyond the capabilities of the gunsight.

The men and the ship moved slowly, with obvious pain.

Aden braced himself against the column. He had no shields of his own to stop the heat or block the frightening resonances that he saw through the sight. He thought they were also visible at the edges of his vision, as when one saw faint stars by looking for them with purposeful indirection. That had been the way the Special Office had looked at everything.

The attendant had not moved. Although it was impossible to know, Aden thought that it was the unicorn's own creation. The other possibility that suggested itself was that the giant was the unicorn's master and creator, now enslaved and drained by the creature and the singular vision it had acquired.

But its power, whether the unicorn's own or stolen, did not stop the ship. Its shields expanded against the tiers of light in proportion to the closing distance between them. The undulating walls and wave fronts stiffened, as if they had suddenly dried out, and long, irregular cracks ate at their fluidity. The fissures spread through the unicorn's power like branches of lighning, all twisting angles and lines through which the blueness of the sky shone with jarring tranquillity.

The fabric of the unicorn's power broke against the ship's defenses. Both its eyes began flicking from side to side, briefly snaring Aden where he hid, pleading for help in the casting of its spells, and then jerking back to the advancing ship.

The men staggered under the weight of the enchantments the beast hurled at them. But the heat and the lights that infused all the hidden spectrums only magnified the ship's progress, muffling its irregularities, blurring its halts and hesitations into the semblance of relentless progress.

Aden pressed himself against the stone, frantically asking why he had to watch this.

The unicorn moved for the first time. It shifted its weight from its front hooves to the rear, apparently trying to find better footing on the paving stones.

It wavered, adjusted its stance again, and then took a step backward. The attendant giant stayed where he was. Only the figures on his skin moved.

A shout came from one or two of the men, and a thin hiss of probing electrons and subatomic particles rushed from the ship to fill up the space from which the unicorn had just stepped, studying the nature of the absence it created as thoroughly as other radiations continued to examine its presence.

The men were walking faster, moving more at right angles to the unicorn rather than toward it. Aden looked through the gunsight and saw globes of shimmering light with lines traced upon them, forming within the ship's dish antennas, and then flying outward against the current of the unicorn's magic, toward the center of the square. Thick ropes of energy followed behind them, using them as anchors. Gradually, they contained and enveloped the enemy's world. And if one had been captured, bound in unimaginable chains, imprisoned in a Chinese box of cages-within-cages, each one confining the wizard in each of the spectrums he chose to occupy—what then could one do with him?

Aden guessed. The hideous fantasies and speculations of the preceding nights, and of the entire time since he had left the Taritan flooded back into his mind.

Everything, except the ship, the men flanking it and the unicorn, was held immobile in huge calipers of light and energy. He barely noticed that the City's pace of decay was speeding up around the square, where the near misses of the ship and the unicorn blasted into the walls and buttressed towers.

The gun was locked against his shoulder. He found a shallow border cut into the column and rested the gun barrel against it. With the bracing and the gun's own internal stabilization systems, the image of the unicorn froze in the sight. It wavered only when rolling currents of heated air billowed between them, making it seem as if they were separated by depths of clear water and the ocean had returned and buried them in the middle of their war.

"You!" The voice was far away. "Ad . . . Aden? Aden! Stop him!" Him? The unicorn? Himself?

The wires burned, inflicting visible patterns of light on his consciousness, trying to reassure him with the familiarity of their pain, trying to distract him from the voice with broken snatches of coherency.

Tiny numbers in red lined the bottom of the gunsight; the unicorn's range was exactly thirty-one meters. The gun spoke to itself and reformulated and redefined its ammunition.

At a range of twenty-eight meters he could see that the unicorn's horn was not made of gold and ebony. There was only a single tapering spiral of gold that held an absolute vacuum within it. It was a vacuum of light as well as of air, warmth, energy, life. It was a spear made from the darkness that was supposed to lie behind the throne of god, the night into which even he would, in time, tumble and be lost. It was an absolute, a thing for which there could be no understanding or comprehension. Perhaps. That was how the gryphon-cavalrymen had thought of themselves.

"Stop! Please! Aden, listen to . . ." Engines rising to his left and boots falling rapidly on the paving stones. The ship was pouring immense amounts of energy onto the square, dissolving the fountain and then drowning the attendant where he stood.

The unicorn focused its own eyes and that of the Office on Aden, twenty-two meters away. The cranial net shrieked inside his skull, speaking a single word that he had never heard before.

The gun fired at the command. His senses, heightened by fear, saw the iridescent bulb, electric blue and white, grow from the muzzle, burning away the skin on his knuckles, exposing nerves and old scar tissue, expanding and transmuting into silver and then into the deep chrome that one sees in polished mirrors. The shell was without mass in four of the spectrums perceptible to the gun, infinite in one, and weighing four, five and eight grams, respectively, in the remaining three.

The unicorn faced directly into its flight. The shell drove into its left eye, shattering the artificial one and then the magical one in back of it.

The gun repeated the sequence. This time the bullet struck the right eye. Aden distantly heard more shouting, hysterical and deafening in the abrupt silence of the wires inside his head.

A wall of energy from the ship swept between him and the unicorn. It fell and shoved him laterally down the length of the arcade.

The unicorn died behind the wall. The energies that held it together erupted through the two bullet wounds, and poisoned all of the lands and universes into which it might have tried to flee and carry on the War.

The burning air whipped itself into a storm and then into hurricane circularities around the unicorn. It rose above the sound of the ship's engines and the cursing of the men's voices. Aden could not tell if he was unconscious or buried under debris. Above him, masonry and metal broke apart with thunderous reports. The ground under him quivered as more buildings disintegrated and fell. To maintain the symmetry of its own conception of the world, the dying unicorn was draining all the magic that remained in the City. Sudden gaps were created which could be filled in only one logical way.

Logical. The mode of death was that of his own world, not of the unicorn's.

At the center of the winds, hidden from him by the ship's last screen, Aden envisioned the part of its horn that was the night acting as a dark polar star for the escape of the creature's soul. Its creator had been powerful enough to have imprisoned that on the unicorn's forehead; the creation of a soul so that the unicorn could follow and serve him after its death would have been comparatively simple.

The horn shriveled, and the life of the unicorn fled into it. Behind it, the magical energies of the creature and those which it had torn loose from the City increased, effloresced and blinded Etridge, Stamp, Grant and Halstead.

They had huddled under the grounded ship for an hour while the unicorn died, unable to move because of the storm it had summoned. While they waited, the winds outside reached four hundred and twenty kilometers an hour and drifting blocks of hard radiation bombarded the ship's armored sides.

It had taken another two hours for the dust to settle. There were no more plasmas spouting from the fountain when they emerged, neither were there any memorialists looking for corpses to eulogize or statues saluting their appearance. The unicorn had taken all the City's magic and hidden it in its own death.

Etridge looked around himself. The afternoon showed them nothing that might have been a recognizable part of a building, so complete was the devastation. Coherency of form remained only in the paving blocks under them and in the ship itself. The cathedral was gone, except for its stairs leading up from the rubble-filled square into blank air. Everything had been crushed and leveled, as if the seven hundred years of war had never happened, as if the wizards had never slaughtered their millions.

Now, Stamp thought, we have only our murderous philosophy and the weapons that articulated it to prove that the enemy had thrown their enchantments against us, or that they ever caused things like Thorn River to have happened.

Anderton reviewed the spectrums. The only thing left was the Special Office man and he directed Etridge to where he lay. Etridge walked stiffly away from the ship.

His initial emotion was self-hatred for not having eliminated the man when he had first been spotted. But he had never thought of the Office as being terribly effective, except in confusing its own personnel—and politicians and theologians when the time was appropriate. The man might have even helped them.

They had intercepted the signals as they were broadcast to the man. The computers had shunted aside any attempt to decode them because it would distract them from their examination of the unicorn, and because they recognized that they were purposely fragmentary and incomplete.

As at Thorn River, Etridge had allowed this Aden to stay, half thinking to see how the energies of magic played against him and the ways they would take him apart. As at Thorn River, he had learned more about the processes of magic than the processes of men. He had discounted the possibilities of Aden's survival and his capacity for action. Being neither committed to his own world nor having fully gone over to the other side, the man obviously existed in a vacuum; nothing lived, Etridge knew, outside of the great counterpositions of rationality and magic, and all the man's actions must therefore be nothing more than futile gestures, deprived of even symbolic meaning.

The man had taken the unicorn from him.

Stamp followed dumbly behind Etridge. They could hear Anderton's voice over the ship's speaker monotonously reciting the absence of extraordinary phenomena in each of the parallel spectrums. The gulls came back over the City, crying to one another, reserving their fishing grounds for when the ocean returned.

Etridge's anger grew inside of him, the rifle glistening where he ran his hands along it. The last gateway had been snatched away from him at the moment of its attainment.

Stamp saw the volcanic light reignited in Etridge's eyes as they neared the man. He was dressed in rags and looked like a beggar from the worst part of any town in either of the enemy worlds.

The air was still thick with powdered masonry and rotted magic, so he could not tell if he smelled as badly as he looked.

"Aden?" Etridge asked with brittle formality.

The man raised his head, looked at them with his one good eye and nodded.

"Special Office?" Etridge went on. Stamp fingered the safety on his rifle uneasily. The cut glass exactitude of his voice indicated shock and insanity.

"I was. It doesn't exist any more." The other man sounded incredibly tired.

"No more than the unicorn does. Now." Etridge bent over, grabbed Aden's filthy tunic with his right hand and easily lifted him to his feet. "But it existed a moment ago. Didn't it? We heard the signals. We saw what this toy of yours did." He let go of the man and grabbed the pistol from his right hand. Etridge stared at it for a second and then hurled it into the rubble. It exploded into gray smoke where it hit.

"The thing is over, sir. We've won." Aden refused to meet their eyes. "Please . . ."

"Name of god I will!" Etridge roared. "You took the unicorn away from me. Blew it up and packed it away in god and history where no one can get it!"

"You couldn't have . . ."

"Then why kill it, Aden?" Etridge had his hand around the man's shirt front again, twisting the cloth and drawing his face closer. "Why the words from your damn Office, or from whatever thing or monster was speaking to you? Why that bastard little gun of yours? Just refugees talking to one another, right? Little, gutless minds the war's used up and thrown away, to bother people like me! That's you, Aden, and your bloody Office! You know that?"

Aden tried to speak but nothing came out. Stamp saw dark recognition spreading over his face, blocking his words. Simultaneously, a mirror image of the same emotion crossed Etridge's face.

Aden tried to tell him about the eye. "The Special Office never was. It closed down . . ."

"It's still open. Just like you. And now that you, all of you've taken the unicorn, I'll tell you what we're going to do!" Etridge paused. He stood there for more than two minutes, looking down into the agent's eye, half of him seeming to wait for some signal to be broadcast to Aden from an antenna at Lake Gilbert or some outpost situated deeply within the terrible regions he wished so passionately to explore and subdue.

"You're so lost in your own language and your precious balancing act between our world and their's that you're half magic yourselves. That's what you'd want, that's what you'd like, isn't it? *Isn't it?"* Aden nodded stupidly to Etridge. "So we're going to follow *you.* Let you go, all of you, and follow you and your goddamn bleeding Special Office! And when you run from us, when you run in the only ways you've taught yourselves, you're going to lead us to and through all of the secrets that beast took with it." Etridge threw Aden backward into the rubble so violently that he almost lost his balance and fell with him.

16

179

THE SIEGE OF WONDER

"We're going to chase your gang through every spectrum, through every dimension and hiding place you run to. You're cripples, Aden! When we move after you, you and your Office'll run, it'll be in directions that we can anticipate. One chase, one segment at a time. You're going to teach us, everything, until we don't need you any more."

Stamp felt a vicious peace and contentment inside of him; his conversion had not come too soon. This way would take longer, but the understanding and the triumph would inevitably be theirs. He knew that it would, both in his own mind and from the way Aden's face passed through shock into a despair so profound that it could only be a reflection of truth.